The Christmas Contradiction

Gwen Hayes

Published by Gwen Hayes, 2015.

This is a work of fiction. Similarities to real people, places, or events are entirely coincidental.

THE CHRISTMAS CONTRADICTION

First edition. November 28, 2015.

Copyright © 2015 Gwen Hayes.

Written by Gwen Hayes.

Don't Stop Believing

The Ogre from the Hill

Simon Powell, the town recluse, only comes to town to deliver firewood and get supplies.

The Book Nerd from the City

Adam Parker moved to the small community to make big changes in his life, but being snowbound with the bearded lumberjack in his rustic cabin was something he'd thought only existed in his fantasies.

A Christmas to Remember

Adam smells like cinnamon and redemption and Simon aches to reignite feelings he'd denied himself for too long But Simon learned long ago that everything he touches gets tainted, and he'll do anything to keep his darkness away from Adam's light.

But Adam has something else on his side—he's been a very good boy this year and all he wants for Christmas is Simon.

Chapter One

THE CRISP AIR SMELLED LIKE snow, and the dark canopy of clouds promised the same. White icicle lights glowed merrily off every shop of downtown Silver Pines, Washington, and green garland wreaths with cheery red bows decorated each lamp post. Simon Powell inhaled deeply. Everything smelled like cinnamon.

He should have just stayed home.

He'd known better. Two days before Christmas was not a good day for him to come down from Ogre Hill. And yes, he was well aware that's what the locals called his home up Bear Mountain Road. Silver Pines was too small, too quaint, and too busy getting ready for the holiday and the impending snow. But he needed supplies and he hadn't spoken to another person in probably too long. That part didn't bother him so much, but he felt a certain responsibility to not become a cliché.

It wasn't that he didn't like people. He just didn't *enjoy* them. Or Christmas.

Or smiling.

"Simon!"

He cringed. He recognized her voice and knew it was bad news. He turned. Slowly. "Stella," he grunted.

She was laden with overflowing gift bags and wore an askew Santa hat. "I was just going to call you."

Not again.

Stella Stone only called for one reason.

"I can't." He pivoted for a getaway.

She stepped up her game and got in front of him, walking backward. "He's blind."

He stopped, closed his eyes, and sighed.

"Please? You're my last hope. He can't be alone right now. It's Christmas. Just until I find him a permanent home. Please, Simon?"

"What am I going to do with a blind puppy, Stella?" But he already knew. Take care of it. Just like he took in all her misfits until she homed them.

He took a couple bags off her arm and walked with her toward her apartment. He hated how easily she wrapped him around her little finger. But it had been that way since he moved to town, and using her connections, she helped him arrange an adoption of a warrior dog when she was only fifteen-years-old. He'd wanted to give a home to a wounded vet like himself, and she'd found him Maya, a Belgian Malinois who suffered severe depression after the loss of her handler on the battlefield. Maya was his best friend now, and they managed well together.

Stella had a gift. And there were few animals in Silver Pines who hadn't been homed by her tenacious, yet soft, heart.

The problem was that if she wasn't trying to match him to a dog, she was trying to set him up on dates. She didn't seem to care if the other guy was straight, though, assuming he had some sort of power to "just turn him." Her words. He appreciated the faith she had in him, but he wasn't really interested in dating, much less "turning" anyone.

He liked being alone just fine.

He got her packages home, promised to stop by the vet's office to pick up Bingo before five, and went back to his errand list as the snow began to fall. He grunted twelve return "Merry Christmases" and one "Happy Holidays." Was there not one store in Silver Pines that didn't play Christmas music?

The library. It would be quiet.

But the library held its own set of challenges.

Actually just one. Adam Parker.

Adam was new to town, taking over the librarian position from Mrs. Patel who'd retired at the age of 76. Simon liked Mrs.

Patel. She didn't care for nonsense. She didn't like small talk. She didn't have a dimple in her right cheek. She didn't wear glasses that perpetually needed to be pushed back onto her nose. She didn't showcase her ass in tight slacks. She didn't have a chuckle that sent an ache low into Simon's stomach.

Simon swallowed hard and forced his scowl into place to discourage unwanted conversation before he opened the door to the library. If the weather forecast was correct, he was going to need several books to get through the next week. Mr. Literary Tightpants could just keep his dimple to himself today.

Adam felt the chill after the door closed. It wasn't the weather, it was the patron.

Simon Powell AKA The Ogre from the Hill

AKA the object of too many unwarranted fantasies since Adam moved to Silver Pines.

He could hardly be blamed. Simon was a rare specimen. All that brawn, so little time. Today, he wore a blue plaid flannel shirt over a heather gray Henley, jeans, work boots, and the requisite glower. The gray beanie looked Portlandy, but it was the dark beard glittering with just a few grays that always made Adam pause for breath. The man knew how to wear a beard.

From the locals, he'd learned that Simon lived alone on the hill and sold firewood for money. A real live lumberjack. Adam pushed his glasses up. He'd never worked with his hands. Growing up, he'd always leaned more toward cerebral pursuits. Moving to the city after college, he hadn't developed any outdoorsy skills, but he could certainly appreciate them. And did he.

Simon nodded what passed as a greeting as he deposited his books into the drop. As he turned toward the stacks, Adam couldn't resist a little goading. "Can I help you find anything in particular today, Simon?"

Simon shook his head. "I don't want to keep you."

God. That voice.

Adam exaggerated a look around at the empty library. "It seems like I have a lull right now." All day. Most days.

Simon shook his head again. "Take a coffee break then. I don't need any help."

"Good idea. How do you take yours? I'll bring you a cup. Unless you prefer tea?"

His solidly muscled mountain man drew his brow in confusion. "I—No."

Adam rounded the counter. "So you like coffee. Cream? Sugar?"

Simon shook his head and grumbled something incoherent, crossing the small library in long strides. Adam assumed black/no sugar and found him in the *L*s. He handed the bewildered recluse the cheeriest holiday cup he could find. Simon scowled at it, but managed a low, "Thanks."

"Holiday plans?" Adam asked, not sure why he wanted to egg the man on so much. He just felt the need to make sure Simon was aware of him.

"No."

"I'll be heading to Moses Lake. I have family there."

Simon paused, lines deepening on his forehead. "You're an idiot if you think you're leaving town. The storm."

"I have four-wheel-drive—"

"You think that's going to help you when you're sailing down a cliff?"

He sounded like he cared. Almost.

Adam leaned against the shelves. The strong coffee combined with the scent of the books and the fresh scent of Simon's soap all coalesced together into what he imagined heaven must smell like. "I don't have family any closer. It's take my chances or be alone.

I've never been alone on Christmas." He hadn't meant to drop his voice at the end there. Last Christmas, he'd been with Blake and probably would have been better off alone. He just couldn't face the emptiness this year.

"Being alone isn't so bad," Simon groused. "Better than being dead at the bottom of a mountain."

Their gazes met over the rims of their coffee cups. It felt to Adam like he'd just been lit up like the town Christmas tree. A jolt of heat and color rushed past his eyes, carols singing through his veins, and he shook himself, remembering where he was and who he was talking to. "I'll let you finish picking out your books."

Adam tried to pin down what he was feeling, but the best he could come up with at that moment was...alive. His heart raced, his skin flushed, and he kept trying to check his reflection in the window behind his desk. It was one thing to have found Simon attractive, it was another to act like a kid with a crush. What was wrong with him? Even if Simon were gay, and he suspected he was, he was obviously not interested in Adam. Simon the Recluse was the exact opposite of what Adam wanted, needed, at this point in his life.

After Blake, he'd realized something very important. He didn't want to just hook up anymore. He was ready to settle down, to devote himself to someone else and be devoted to in return. Hell, he was even beginning to think he wanted kids someday. Possibly. And if he couldn't have the real thing, he was tired of faking it. He'd taken a job as far away from city life and the singles scene as he could find. True, finding his soul mate might be harder in a small town, but the pace felt right. He'd just ...known... he needed to be here the first time he'd visited Silver Pines.

But someone who obviously didn't like people, who took exception to having to share something as simple as a cup of coffee, was not the kind of person Adam needed to be hanging around with.

He intended to be all business when Simon brought his books up. It was Simon who palmed Adam's arm over the counter. "Don't chance the roads tonight. It wouldn't be safe going over the passes even if you had left hours ago. Don't risk it."

He looked down at the beefy hand, the rough calluses, the breadth of his palm. *Breathe, dude.* He followed the line of Simon's wrist to his forearm, over the biceps pulling the sleeves of his shirt tautly across it. He continued his perusal over the wide shoulder, pausing on the skin just under the beard, then dragged his gaze up to Simon's eyes, knowing better than to stop on his lips. Staring at his lips would be more dangerous than the slick roads over the Cascades.

"I'll turn around if they close the pass."

There was a long moment between them. They were taking measure. He wondered what they looked like together, the beast and the dorky librarian. His glasses felt very heavy on his nose, his sweater too tight. He waited, wondering what this man would say or do next. Retreat? Make a pass? Beat him up for getting his gay germs on him?

"Silver Pines is too small that nobody offered you a meal on Christmas. Take someone up on it." Then he pulled his hand away.

Retreat then. He should have figured.

"What about you? Why be alone on a holiday? Tell me nobody offered *you* a meal on Christmas and I'll forgive your library fines." Because it was a safe bet in this town. Simon would have been invited to at least five Christmas dinners.

That heavy hand went to his chin, stroking his beard thoughtfully. "I'm not good company. Wouldn't want to subject anyone to that."

It poked a hole in Adam's heart to hear him say it. To think it of himself. They were mostly strangers, but Adam couldn't imagine not wanting to subject himself to Simon's company. He felt like he would be eagerly scooping up every minute he spent with Simon Powell for the years to come. He'd probably sadly relive each interaction, growing old and alone, pining in earnest for these little scraps of attention from a library patron who would never think of him outside these walls.

Pathetic.

"Wait a minute? What library fines?" Simon interrupted his maudlin thoughts.

Adam leaned across the counter between them, within smelling distance. God. It was just soap. Simon wasn't the cologne type, but it was amazing. "You owe $8.10 from eight years ago." Simon's eyes were the darkest brown he'd ever seen.

Simon dropped his head and screwed his features into the "you've got to be kidding me" pose. "Mrs. Patel told me I didn't have to pay those."

"Well, she didn't erase them from your account. Besides, there's a new librarian in town." He winked before he could stop himself.

One side of Simon's mouth quirked up in a small tic. If Adam hadn't been so focused, staring and in the man's space, he'd have missed it because it was gone as fast as it came. "Is that right? And you make your own laws then?"

"Just doing my job, sir."

He went back to scanning the books out, but felt Simon's gaze on him like heat. He pushed the books across their shared space, sorry that it was already over and wondering how many times he'd rerun the simple conversation, exaggerating the parts he could pretend were Simon flirting with him.

"Don't leave." Simon didn't say goodbye. Just took his books and left.

But Adam heard "don't leave" in his head for the rest of the afternoon.

Chapter Two

IT HAD BEEN A LONG time since snow had fallen this hard, this fast. Simon wished he'd gone to town earlier so he'd have been home with a full belly by now. Maybe he should have skipped the library. No. But maybe skipped the errands after the library.

The road was treacherous and the going slow. He slowed down even more when he saw the taillights of a car clearly stuck in a ditch on the other side of the road. He grumbled as he pulled over. Fools. Part of him panicked. Just a twinge really. What if it was the librarian? What if he were hurt?

A man was in the snow, trying in vain to push the car out by himself. Which of course he would never accomplish. He knew it was Adam as soon as he got out of his truck. He probably had known from the minute he saw the lights. The ache in his gut told him just like the one in his leg warned him before it rained.

"Simon," Adam rubbed his hands together. His bare hands.

Simon rolled his eyes and ripped off his gloves before he threw them at Adam. "You injured?"

Adam shook his head. "No. Just cold and stupid, thanks." He threw the gloves back. Petulant ass. "I started to go and realized I'd never make it. I turned around, but even getting back to town is rough now."

But Simon saw the blood above his eyebrow. "Hell, you're bleeding."

"It's just a scratch."

Just a scratch. God, what if he'd made it to the pass before he went off road? Did the man not think? "Did you call for help yet?"

"No...I...no. I was hoping to get back on the road, but I guess that's not going to happen."

"Go warm up in the cab of my truck." He didn't want to think about why he was so damned mad. His hands started shaking the minute he'd seen the blood.

He sized up the situation and realized the car was staying put for the night. There was one tow truck in town and it was probably busy. Best save it for emergencies. They were closer to his cabin than town, but he hadn't had company in a very long time. For a reason.

Hell. He needed to get a good look at the "just a scratch" or he'd never sleep tonight anyway.

He stalked back to his truck and got in.

"You have a puppy in here," Adam said. "That was unexpected."

Bingo, the six-week-old golden lab mix was burrowed into Adam's neck. A quivering mess. Designed to manipulate humans into doing exactly what Adam was doing.

"I'm watching him until he can be adopted. He's blind." Adam looked at Simon like he'd never seen him before. Was Simon really that scary? The Ogre from the Hill? "Plus, I needed something to eat for Christmas dinner."

Adam chuckled. "My car?"

"Not tonight."

"I'll hike back into town."

Simon shook his head and put the truck in gear.

"I don't want you to go back down. It's already treacherous enough. I'll walk. I'll be fine."

"I'm not taking you back to town. At least not yet."

"Then where are you taking me?" His tone made Simon grimace. Adam was flirting with Simon.

Damn it.

"Home." Silence. "I want to have a look at that cut. Make sure you don't need medical attention. I don't think you should be alone. In case you have a concussion."

"You're taking me to your house?"

Simon grunted a yes. Hoping he wouldn't have to keep talking. Because, probably, he could take Adam back to town and get home again just fine. But he didn't want to. He wanted to bring Adam to his cabin. Which made no sense. Simon didn't like people in his space. But the idea of taking Adam to his apartment...of Adam being alone in town while Simon was alone on the hill...made him feel hollow.

They didn't speak the rest of the drive. Which was fine. He wasn't exactly a conversationalist. Adam probably had lots to say. He was thoughtful, intelligent. Simon liked to read, but he had an idea that books were more to Adam than entertainment. Like he needed to be surrounded by big ideas to thrive.

Simon pushed back any ideas of his own he might be having. Especially of Adam.

Simon watched the younger man carefully when he let Adam into the cabin. Watched to see if Adam's face fell. If he hated the thought of being stuck up here in the woods with Simon.

What he saw, instead, made his heart skip a beat, made it radiate a strange warmth. Adam was impressed. Maybe even amazed. He looked around the room, his eyes growing bigger. "You...you built this house, I heard. By yourself?"

"A little bit at a time."

"It's gorgeous."

Simon tamped down his feelings. "I'll get the first aid kit." Simon had notched the logs with his own ax, hand-peeled the porch rails. All the time and effort he could no longer give to people, he gave to his home. He was proud, too damned proud. And he didn't want to examine why it was necessary that Adam liked it.

"What do I do with this dog?" Adam asked to Simon's back.

"Just hold him for a few minutes. I'll get a fire going after we check out your wound."

When he got back into his living area, Adam was sitting in his reading chair holding Bingo on his lap while Simon's other dog, Maya, sniffed the pup curiously.

"Should I be worried about these two?" Adam asked.

"No. Maya won't do anything I don't tell her to do."

Adam raised his brow, but didn't add to the thought out loud. He definitely thought something, though.

Simon twisted the neck of his reading lamp to get a better look at the cut. Carefully, he removed Adam's glasses and set them on the end table. It was strange to see something of someone else in a space only Simon had ever occupied. Maybe he liked it.

Maybe he didn't.

Carefully, he cleaned the wound, relieved it was, indeed, just a scratch.

"Well, doc, am I gonna live?"

"You won't need stitches. But you're going to have a good bruise and that goose egg isn't going to feel very good. You let me know if you get dizzy or nauseous."

"I know the signs of concussion, and I will let you know." The tension in his voice made Simon realize he was being patronizing.

They were close. Too close. Close enough to see how green Adam's eyes were. Like an apple. The squirming puppy between them broke his concentrated effort of memorizing Adam's face, and he backed away. "I'll get a fire going."

But first, he went into his room and found some dry clothes. The guy hadn't dressed for the weather—another thing he'd like to berate him for. You don't travel mountain passes in city clothes. He should have had on warm boots, heavy jeans, a waterproof coat. And gloves, for God's sake.

Simon took the puppy from Adam and handed him the sweats with no comment before Simon went about rekindling the fire in the stove. Adam didn't close the bedroom door behind him, so Simon could hear the clothes coming off. Simon tried to mask the sound with making fire as loud as he could, but he couldn't mask his thoughts.

How long had it been since he'd touched someone? Since he'd pulled the clothes off a man, revealing skin and muscle and...

"What is it that smells so good?" Adam popped out of the room talking.

"I put a stew on before I left today. We'll eat next."

"You made stew?"

"I live alone on a mountain, Adam. I have to cook or I don't eat."

"It just seems...I don't know...homey. Do you need me to do something with the puppy?"

Simon rose. "She'll get stew also. After we eat."

"You feed your animals people food."

"Cooking for one is hard. I share my meals with Maya, though she chews more bones than I do. As long as it isn't junk food, she eats what I eat for dinner."

They went to the kitchen where he ladled stew into bowls for the dogs so it would cool while they ate.

"I also cook for one." Moving around Simon's kitchen as if he had always been there, Adam pulled two more bowls out of the cupboard and plucked the ladle out Simon's hand, winking before he served them the stew. "I end up making a lot of sandwiches so I don't waste so much."

Simon put the pup into Maya's dog bed and opened a bottle of wine, praying Adam wouldn't notice they drank it out of tumblers because he had no wine glasses. At least he had wine. He wasn't a total barbarian. "Maybe you should get a dog."

"Maybe I should get a friend."

A friend. The word hung in the air between them. Surely Adam had heard that Simon was gay by now. While he'd never run into prejudice in their small town, neither had anyone shied away from using his sexual preference as a conversation starter.

"A dog is a good friend," Simon finally said.

As they sat, Adam agreed about the dog and tried a little small talk. Simon found himself responding with one-word answers. Being a dick. Which he was good at. Because small talk, he was not good at.

"Simon, do I make you uncomfortable?"

He shook his head. "Not you specifically. I'm not good with people."

Adam swallowed his wine, drawing Simon's attention to Adam's throat as he swallowed. Shit. It was a mistake bringing him here.

"You don't seem to *dislike* people. Most of the town is quite fond of you."

"I don't dislike anyone. I just, I'm not comfortable. I like to be alone."

"Do you ever get lonely?"

"No."

"Are you lying?"

He wanted to get angry at this intrusion from this man who thought he knew Simon better than he knew himself. But he'd invited the guy to his fortress of solitude, he'd brought him here with no way to leave in a snowstorm. He'd instigated this from the start, hadn't he? He could have taken Adam home. It wasn't as if ten years on a mountain hadn't forced him to drive in worse conditions than what they'd faced on the road an hour ago.

He was lonely. He hadn't known it, though, until he'd faced the possibility of not bringing Adam home with him tonight. He was lonely *for* Adam.

And that pissed him off.

"Do you want me to lie to you?"

Adam set his glass down. "No, of course not."

"You one of those who believes the truth sets you free?"

"I try to be honest at all times, but especially with myself. Are you saying you don't believe the truth sets you free?"

"Nothing sets you free." Simon got up to take care of the dogs. He could feel Adam's eyes on him. Watching him, assessing him. His leg started to ache and that pissed him off, too. Not the pain, but the idea that he didn't want Adam to see him limp.

Adam cleared the table. "I'm sorry to have inconvenienced you so much tonight. My overnight bag is still in my car. I hadn't thought to grab it."

Simon responded with a grunt rather than give voice to what he wanted to say. That it wasn't an inconvenience. That he'd practically kidnapped Adam to bring him here.

"I don't have any of my things."

"I have an extra toothbrush. Whatever you need tonight."

Adam grabbed his arm, forcing him to turn around. "Why do you have a guest toothbrush if you don't want guests?"

"Don't read too much into it. I bought an extra one when they were on sale." He looked down at the hand on his arm. It was smooth, not marred with nicks and calluses like his. He'd noticed earlier that Adam's fingernails were clean, trimmed, well cared for. He was so different. He must think of Simon like a beast. Like they all did.

But the hand was still there. Still on his arm. And he was wearing Simon's clothes. Why was that a turn on?

"Does it bother you that I'm gay, Simon?"

He met Adam's eyes, sure his own were wide. "No," he choked out.

"Does it bother you that I'm attracted to you?" He squeezed Simon's arm. It wasn't sexual, but Simon felt the pull deep inside as if it were. Adam may have been bookish, but he wasn't weak. He'd give as good as he got and the idea of where else he might grasp Simon so firmly started a riot in Simon's body.

"No," Simon lied. Because it bothered him very much. It made him feel like there were possibilities he hadn't considered before, and he didn't want to. Shouldn't want to. He was set in his ways. Used to the way things were. The way he felt around Adam was not welcome.

There was a moment. A moment that Simon knew he was an inch from being whole again. An inch from reaching out to another human being. Just an inch. If he could close it, if he could brave one goddamned inch, he could have a life again. He knew it. He felt it. Life was right there, blazing in the eyes of the town librarian. A man who wasn't afraid of him. A man who Simon knew, knew in his bones, was everything he'd ever needed. Ever wanted.

Adam was right there. He smelled like cinnamon and redemption and Simon ached to touch him. To run his fingers over the scrape of stubble on his cheeks. To pull him into a kiss. To pour his loneliness out and rely on someone else to fill him back up with feelings he'd denied for too long.

He closed his eyes. "I need to take care of the dogs."

And he left his heart's desire in the kitchen because his heart didn't deserve what it wanted.

Chapter Three

SIMON OPENED ONE EYE, AWARE that something woke him up. Not a sound...a scent.

Bacon?

He rolled out of bed, eying the cane next to it and declining silently.

Maya, not being a dummy, was already in the kitchen, as was Bingo who'd been let free of his crate. But it was Adam that had all their attention—especially Simon's.

Still wearing Simon's sweats but not the T-shirt, not any shirt, Adam was frying bacon. The play of muscles over his back had Simon clenching and unclenching his fists. The way the sweatpants rode so low on his hips...

"Merry Christmas Eve," Adam said over his shoulder. "Breakfast is almost ready. Have some coffee."

No one had ever cooked in his kitchen but Simon. No one had moved around his home like he belonged. Simon warily moved to the coffee maker feeling like he might around a wild animal he didn't want to scare away. *Don't leave.*

"The snow is...well, it's worse. We got dumped on last night." Adam flipped a piece of French toast.

Simon looked out the window, and sure enough, everything was white, silent, and perfect.

"I let the dogs out. No puppy accidents in the crate. I'm impressed."

Simon didn't let himself turn around. Just drank his coffee and stared out the window only half listening to Adam as he talked about the dogs, the stove, the weather—he just kept talking and Simon kept staring, not yet having said a single word.

It was hard to absorb all this chatter so early. He was used to quiet mornings. Quiet afternoons. Quiet evenings.

"You don't have a TV."

At that, Simon finally turned and wished he hadn't. Adam had plated two breakfasts at his little table. The scene was homey and serene and so out of his range of normal he thought he might have an anxiety attack. Something he hadn't had in years.

"I have a TV in my room for DVDs. I don't have cable or satellite."

Adam, shirtless Adam, took a seat and poured the syrup over his plate. Sticky, sweet syrup. The things he could do with—

"Are you always so talkative in the mornings?" Adam asked, interrupting Simon's thoughts.

Simon sat, quickly to avoid an embarrassing show of where his thoughts had gone. "You didn't have to cook for me."

Adam looked up and smiled, the dimple winking at Simon from under a light scruff. Oh hell.

"You rescued me from the snow, got me dry and warm, fed me, and gave me a place to sleep. The least I could do is make you breakfast. I don't have too many meals in my repertoire, basically breakfast and sandwiches."

Because breakfast was something Adam would make for his own overnight guests. Simon closed his eyes as he thought of him making French toast for another man in another kitchen in a whole other life. A life apart from Simon because everyone's lives were apart from Simon. And that was how he wanted it, wasn't it?

"Simon?" Their gazes clashed across the small table. "Would you like some syrup?"

Syrup. Or more? Was it his imagination or had he heard an offer in there? Simon was shit with people, but he hadn't always been. Once upon a time, he'd known how to navigate a world with friends and lovers. Potential lovers. He'd even given his heart—to his job, his brothers, his country…to Michael.

"No," he answered, and went about cutting his plain bread.

Adam was getting nowhere fast. After breakfast, he dressed in yesterday's clothes and told Simon he was headed back down to his car. Which, apparently, was not a good idea, according to Simon. The man of very few words.

He couldn't have made it plainer that he wanted Adam to stay, but at the same time, refused to acknowledge that he wanted him there at all.

His phone was almost dead, so he made sure his family knew he wasn't making the drive today either and turned it off. His charger was still in his car, so he'd just be stuck without. Simon informed him the internet was down, so checking the roads and weather on Simon's computer was out too.

So he was staying. For a while, at least. He spent most of the morning watching Simon work with Bingo, teaching him sit. The patience and gentleness he showed the blind puppy was amazing. Not that he'd expected less, but the gruff mountain man who would rather eat dry French toast than acknowledge that he wanted maple syrup was a very complex man, indeed.

He also had a good book collection, so they sat in front of the fire and read for an hour. The dogs content, the fire warm, the company—actually not bad considering they barely spoke.

There was something there. Adam felt it and knew Simon did as well. What he didn't know was why he was so reluctant to experience it. He was, in no uncertain terms, gay.

Every time he closed his eyes, he saw Simon sitting across from him at breakfast, naked need in his eyes. What would have happened if he'd closed the distance between them, had made the first move? He didn't usually. He'd always liked to be chased. But then, he usually dated men who liked to do the chasing. He wondered what kind of men Simon liked. Was he the hunter or the prey? He couldn't imagine either scenario as Simon couldn't play reluctant or coy for a million dollars, but nor was he slick enough to hunt in the forest that made up Adam's dating world. His old world anyway.

He closed his book since he was rereading the same passage over and over.

"You don't have a tree."

Simon looked up from his book. "There's a forest outside the window."

"A Christmas tree, Simon." He looked around. "You don't have any Christmas decorations at all." Though he'd seen a stack of opened cards on the computer desk. Simon might be a recluse, but people cared about him.

"I couldn't do better than what's already outside. How often do we get a white Christmas?"

"Let's go get a small one and bring it in."

Simon grunted his dissent.

"Come on." He reached for a connection between them. "I'm supposed to be at my aunt's today. My boisterous family all around, a tree decorated from floor to ceiling. My aunt has 109 snow globes, you know." Another grunt. "I'm a bit homesick," he lied, but only a little. "It doesn't feel like Christmas."

Simon rolled his eyes. "You'll have to change again. Your fancy library clothes won't hold up to the snow and cold."

Adam laughed. "My fancy library clothes? Are you seventy-years-old now? Fancy, my ass."

Simon narrowed his eyes, that dark brow furrowing. It was just delicious. "Let me get you some sensible clothes and we'll go hunt you down a tree."

Simon's voice was gruff, but his movements were quick and light. He wanted to get a tree. He wanted to lighten up. He was pretending to be a curmudgeon. Adam wondered what he could do to keep him in this state and decided he'd just continue to poke at the bear.

They trudged through the snow for an hour, Simon negating every tree Adam suggested. When he stopped at one taller than himself and assessed it carefully, Adam couldn't quell his surprise. "This is not a small tree. I was thinking you might like just a bit of Christmas, but this is not a bit. This is...will this fit in your living room?"

Simon slid Adam a glance that stole his breath. His dark eyes were twinkling. The lines around his eyes crinkled as he smiled. "Are you worried about carrying it back? The exercise will be good for you. You probably spend too much time inside with all those books."

Fuck me. He's smiling. Adam's stomach took a free fall to his knees.

Suddenly, the minor crush he'd carried morphed into something a little more powerful. A little more dangerous. Adam deliberately brushed against Simon when he walked around the tree, assessing it. "You're not compensating for anything here, are you? Big tree...big truck..."

Simon chuckled. "I guarantee I am not compensating for anything."

Adam's mouth went completely dry. And then the snow began to fall again, assuring them of more time trapped together. He couldn't have been any happier about that unless someone slapped a big red bow on the burly lumberjack in front of him and told him to have his way.

Chapter Four

SIMON LOOKED AROUND THE ROOM and didn't recognize his life.

Adam was currently threading a line of popcorn around the tree that fit just fine in his living room, thank you very much. Christmas music, yes really, was playing on his stereo. He was drinking some sort of hot toddy that Adam invented in his kitchen, and he'd just laughed...out loud even...about a story Adam told him about the live Nativity scene from earlier that week.

He was, for the first time in ten years, sorry he hadn't gone to the town tradition featuring children as the principal players in the manger.

He didn't have much interaction with children. Not like Adam. "You like kids."

Adam shrugged. "Well, yeah. I was the children's librarian for a while before I came here. Here in Silver Pines, we just have one librarian to rule them all."

Simon stroked Maya absently. He could see Adam surrounded by kids at story time. But if he liked it so much, why take on Silver Pines Library? There were fewer children in town than he was probably used to. "Why did you move here? Why give up the city?"

"I was ready for a change." There was more there. He'd hinted at a loneliness earlier. But it was none of Simon's business.

Adam stepped back from the tree and assessed. Popcorn, cranberries, pine cones, and a few paper decorations Adam had cut out from Simon's Christmas cards. It wasn't much. Nothing glittered or lit up. But it was a fine tree.

It was starting to get dark outside, and the power had winked off and on a few times. He should go out and get another few armfuls of wood, but the house was cozy and while he hadn't expected to like it that way, he felt very content. Too content to go back into the cold.

Adam joined him on the couch. "What do you think?"

"It looks great. Really."

"I'm guessing by your lack of decorations that this isn't the only year you haven't had a tree."

"I haven't had a Christmas tree since I left home to join the Navy." His mom had stopped asking him to come home for the holidays about five years ago. He still visited once or twice a year, but not during the holidays.

"Why?"

"I moved a lot when I was active. I needed to be ready to head out at any time as a SEAL."

Adam's shock was painted all over his features. Then he smiled. "A SEAL huh? I've never known one before. I think I must be the only one in town that knows or I'd have heard all about it by now."

"They know I was injured in the service, but they don't know which branch."

"Navy SEAL. Not an easy gig."

Simon shook his head. "It was hard, but I liked it." *I was good at it.*

"I'm trying to picture you clean shaven. And doing push-ups."

"I still do push-ups every day."

He didn't miss the look in Adam's eye. It was more than interest. It was more than flirting. Simon's heart beat harder, his blood rushed stronger. The stared at each other, the moment sexually charged. And more. Something about the Adam made Simon want to be a better man. A stronger man. Not push-up strong. Simon wanted to be the kind of person Adam respected. Maybe even needed.

But no, he couldn't be that. Not for Adam. Not for anyone.

Adam seemed to notice the change in Simon, regarding him carefully. "So, you didn't set down roots while you were in the Navy. But after?"

"After I got out," Simon focused on the amber color of his drink, "I wasn't in the mood to decorate."

As soon as he'd let the words tumble from him mouth, he knew Adam wouldn't let that go.

"How long have you been out, Simon?"

"Twelve years."

"And you've been in Silver Pines for ten?"

Simon nodded. He should go outside. He needed to cut this conversation short because he knew where it was going and he didn't want to look back. Didn't want to reopen the wounds.

"Simon. What happened?"

He couldn't. He just couldn't. Nor could he get up, it seemed.

Adam moved closer to him on the couch and set his drink on the coffee table. Slowly, he covered Simon's hand with his own, squeezing it in support.

Simon's heart stilled. It certainly hadn't been ten years since he'd had sex, he was a recluse not a monk, but it had been fifteen years since someone had held his hand. Adam picked it up and threaded their fingers together. Simon did not pull away, even as the rush of his heartbeat drowned out the music. Drowned out everything.

"Tell me."

He wasn't sure sound would come out, but he opened his mouth anyway. "I was injured. Operation Enduring Freedom."

"That's not why you live like Shrek. *Tell* me."

Simon leaned his head onto the backrest and looked up at the ceiling. "Why is this important to you?"

Without letting go of his hand, Adam shifted until he was kneeling on the floor in front of Simon. He put his other hand on Simon's knee and waited. What was he doing there? So handsome and open and the scariest thing Simon could picture. Comfort. Acceptance. Would he even know what to do with that?

He owed Adam the respect of looking him in the eye, but when he did, he got lost again. There were only ten years or so between them, most likely. But an entire world all the same.

"You don't want to hear my sob story. It's Christmas, let's be merry."

Adam picked up Simon's other hand and brought it to his cheek, kissing the inside of Simon's wrist. A shudder of bliss racked him. And it was such an innocent touch. "Adam..."

"Tell. Me."

He could steer this another way. He didn't have to open a vein and spill out all over this moment. He could lean into Adam right now, take a kiss. Take more. His eyes drifted to his mouth. But no. A kiss would undo him more than the truth.

"My boyfriend got sick."

Like a cat, Adam kept rubbing his cheek into Simon's palm. And he waited. He hadn't shocked him with either his sexual preference or his confession. *Sick* and *boyfriend* usually meant one thing.

"It was 2001. Don't ask; don't tell. And I hadn't told anyone even though my team was, well, they were my brothers. But Michael got sick in '01. Cancer. A very progressive one. And I was in Afghanistan. They didn't let you out for sick *buddies*." Fuck. The thought of calling Michael his *buddy* was like stabbing an icepick into his heart. "Special Ops teams were busy fighting the Taliban. I couldn't leave."

"Michael was more than just a boyfriend," Adam suggested.

"I loved him. I thought we were going to make a life together. That we had all the time in the world. And he died a world away from me in '02." Simon blinked back the tears. It was so long ago, but the pain as fresh as yesterday. "I lost it when I found out. I was gutted. My team asked me over and over what was wrong, and when I wouldn't tell them, they got me drunk until I finally did."

He closed his eyes, remembering the bite of Tequila when it went down, but more when it came back up. He hadn't touched it since.

"I told them about Michael, that I was gay, and then we got the shit bombed out of us before anyone could react. I took shrapnel to my knee, but I was still getting around somehow—adrenalin mostly. But my buddy, Fracker, he wasn't so lucky." He could still smell the blood. "I tried to pick him up, but he wouldn't let me touch him because I was bleeding."

"He was afraid of your blood," Adam repeated.

Simon grunted. "More afraid of getting AIDS than bleeding out in the sand. Like maybe I'd said that it was cancer to cover up the real reason Michael died." Simon pulled his hand away from Adam's face. "I stayed with him, figuring we'd both die there. He told me...he told me God was punishing me for being a gay."

"Jesus, Simon."

"He said I was a liar for not telling them all this time. That I deserved what was coming, but he didn't know what he'd done to deserve it too. That his blood was on my hands. And I sat there in the hole with him while he told me I needed to repent my sins. That I needed to die clean. God hates homos, he said. And he told me all about it until he gurgled on his own blood and died."

Adam placed both Simon's hands on his face, bringing him back to the present. "Simon, he was wrong. You know that."

"He was a bigot, yes I know. And I didn't repent, mostly because I don't believe in God. But when a man would rather die than be tainted by touching you? When—"

"Stop. Just stop."

He tried to move away. "I need to get more firewood."

"Do you believe I deserve to die because I am gay? That I am worth less as a human being because I'm a queer?"

Simon winced at the word. "No. Stop saying that."

"Then why do you let the words of a bigot control how you live thirteen years later? Why do you cut yourself off? So you won't taint anyone else? Would Michael want you to take the blame for a disease you didn't even have?"

"Stop." He pulled at Adam's wrists, trying to remove him but failing. How could he explain to someone who had never been a SEAL what it was like? He couldn't. There were not words for the relationship, though brother came close. Losing Fracker the same day he lost Michael had dropped the bottom from his world. And then, when he'd gotten out of the hospital, he had nothing of the life he knew. No military career thanks to the shrapnel. No one to die for anymore. And no one to live for either. "I'm done talking."

"You deserve to be loved. You deserve to give love."

Adam didn't understand. "I'm not ashamed of being gay."

"No, you're ashamed of being alive."

"Let me up." He couldn't bear it any longer. The weight of the past was too heavy, it would suffocate them both if he didn't get some air.

"Look at me."

Simon set a scowl to his face, the one that always worked at keeping people away. But instead of releasing him, Adam pulled Simon closer and kissed him.

Just once. A whisper across his lips.

Then he backed away. "I'm not sorry that I'm here instead of with my family. This day with you has been one of the best I've had. I like you, Simon. A lot. I think you're sexy and kind and intelligent. I think, if you let someone in, you could also be happy." Adam paused, waiting for affirmation that would never come from Simon. Because he couldn't access that part of himself anymore. "I'm sorry that you lost someone you loved and that your buddy let you down. Because that is what happened, Simon. He let *you* down. Not the other way around. But you need to pull the thorn out of your paw now, or let someone help you do it.

What you are doing up here on this hill is not living. It's not honoring the man you loved. It's not making invisible amends because you are miserable and think you deserve it."

And then he got up and closed himself in the bathroom.

Outside, breathing in the fresh air and pine of the forest, all Simon could taste was cinnamon.

Chapter Five

THE POWER HAD ITS LAST hurrah and still Simon hadn't come in. Adam had watched him from the window earlier as he split wood for one of the ominous piles all over the yard. It was like watching someone dance. The precision, the flex of muscle, the choreographed movements. He was so graceful, yet the most masculine of beasts. But it was dark and the exterior lighting no longer had power and Simon still didn't come in.

A generator roared to life, bringing with it the fridge and a few lights. Well-prepared Simon. Adam went about lighting the kerosene lamps in the living area. It was even better this way. Like a cocoon. Nearly dark, firelight and flame throwing shadows and heat. Adam, the city boy that he was, never realized how much he'd like a place like Simon's. How much he liked Simon.

Before he spilled his secrets, Simon had been surprising Adam all day. The gruff exterior hid so much from the world. Beneath it, Simon was funny even as he was serious. He was charming even as he was bearish. He was—

The door opened, and with it the wind and the bear himself interrupted Adam's thoughts. He was dusted in white like a Yeti for God's sakes

Adam crossed the room. "I was just about to come looking for you."

Simon grunted as he dropped an armload of wood into the box next to the stove.

"You must be freezing. Why didn't you wear a coat?" Without questioning why or how Simon would react, Adam began unbuttoning the red and black flannel he'd worn over his long underwear. "You're soaked."

Simon pushed his hands away. "I can't chop wood wearing a coat. Gets in the way." Simon's own frozen fingers seemed to be getting in the way of his buttons.

"Let me help you," Adam insisted, finishing what Simon struggled with. "There is plenty of wood all over the place around here. You didn't need to split more in the freezing cold. I can hear the wind from in here. You're so…" He peeled the shirt over Simon's shoulders.

"I'm so…?"

Simon had stopped fighting him, and a new tension built. Something had changed. The air crackled with it and an ache in his groin began to radiate through his body.

"Finish your thought, librarian. I'm so…grouchy? Surly? Impossible? Ill-mannered…bad tempered—"

Adam laid a hand on Simon's chest. Felt the hard muscles tighten under his hand. "You're so challenging. Exciting. Provocative—"

With his beefy body, Simon pushed Adam against the wall, hands resting on either side of Adam's head. "Do you know what you are getting into? What you're flirting with?" He rolled his hips so the hard length of him was pushed into Adam. Then he leaned in, his beard brushing against Adam's cheek as he lowered his voice and octave and spoke into his ear. "Is this what you want?"

Adam shivered. "I want you, Simon. Whatever and however much of you I can get."

Simon groaned and took Adams lips. Sampling lightly, tasting, teasing. The kisses kept him off balance in the masculine cage Simon had made of his body. Was Simon holding back or was he just trying to drive Adam crazy? As the kisses veered away from Adam's mouth to his cheek, his chin, Adam clenched. He wanted more. Needed more.

"Simon," he pleaded.

His answer was a grunt and a push of Simon's pelvis so that Adam was cradling him where he needed him most. But still, the kisses were soft, fleeting. Simon was killing him. And Adam would willingly die a thousand deaths.

Adam arched his chest, trying to touch as much of Simon as he could. He braced his hands on Simon's shoulders for support, and when the kisses got close to his mouth again, Adam dove in for more. He opened his mouth, and Simon slipped his tongue inside, mating his mouth. God, Adam nearly exploded right then. There were too many sensations to track properly. The unsatisfying, yet wholly necessary pressure of Simon against his cock. The rasp of his beard. The hot, wet heat of his mouth. The smell of winter and pine and that god damned soap that enveloped them both. He couldn't get close enough. Would never get close enough. Hell.

He had no idea what he was flirting with, and Simon had been right to warn him. He'd never felt so much at once before. They weren't even naked.

Something he needed to remedy soon or he'd go out of his mind.

He swept his hands down Simon's torso until they met the hem of his long underwear, and then they went under. Skin, finally. Simon was a big man, but it was all stocky muscle wrapped in satin. Adam pushed one hand up his chest, the thatches of hair silky and thick against his hand. Simon growled when Adam found a flat nipple and pinched. The growl flipped Adam inside out, and he pushed Simon back enough to get the room he needed to take that shirt off.

With help, Simon was naked first and then they attacked Adam's clothes. As each inch of skin was revealed, another piece of Adam fell into place. Hands and tongues did all the talking, and by some unspoken command, they both avoided touching each other where they ached the most.

Not yet. But soon. God help him, soon.

Simon was big everywhere and Adam couldn't help but stare at him until Simon smiled and pulled him into another rough kiss.

Stumbling to the bedroom, they landed in a heap of limbs on Simon's big bed. The beast had dragged him into his lair, and Adam was profoundly ready to be a sacrifice. Simon pulled back and a relaxed grin stole his features.

"You're still wearing your glasses." Carefully, almost reverently, Simon pulled them off and placed them on the bedside table.

The action seemed to slow their crazed, uninhibited race to get to the good stuff, but before Adam could lament the cooled passion, Simon resumed the soft kisses, starting at Adam's forehead and working his way down. Slowly, languidly, and with a reserve that had Adam taut as a rubber band. He was going to die. He knew it.

"Easy," Simon placated. As if Adam were an animal in distress. And he was. He reached for Simon, but with swift and powerful ease, Simon pinned his hands to the bed. "Don't rush me, librarian."

Adam moaned, but when Simon began to follow each kiss with his tongue, Adam stilled. Waiting for Simon's mouth on him was the ultimate frustration, punishment...pleasure. The beard added a dimension of sensation he hadn't known he'd been missing as Simon used his whole face to create erogenous zones over Adam's entire body.

The low rumble of Simon's groans let Adam know he was enjoying torturing Adam as much as Adam was enjoying being tortured. Simon worked his way back up his body, still ignoring Adam's aching cock as he hovered over his body just enough to tease.

"You seem tense," Simon said as he kissed the cord of Adam's neck.

Now he gets a sense of humor.

"Touch me," Adam pleaded.

"I am touching you," Simon answered before his bit Adam's earlobe.

Adam arched, pushing his pelvis into Simon's and they both moaned and started grinding their hips harder, the pleasure so intense Adam thought he might pass out. Their bodies vibrating against each other, Simon let go of one of Adam's hands and cupped his cheek so they were looking at each other. Simon's eyes were dark with lust. Adam almost came just by looking into them. He was in too deep now. There was no going back to life before he found himself in Simon's bed.

Adam used his now free hand to anchor Simon's hip so he could rub against him harder. Simon growled, his voice a low rumble, beastlike and so exciting. "You're so impatient. I want to make this last," he complained. "Why can't you behave?"

"Next time. Next time, I'll behave," Adam promised. "This time I need you. Now. I feel like I've been waiting forever for you."

Adam stopped talking, worried that he'd said too much. That Simon would put a stop to this now. Instead, Simon captured his mouth in a kiss, his tongue delving into Adam's mouth while he pressed his body against Adam. Simon felt so good, so right.

"I'm going to give you everything you want tonight," Simon rasped. "I'm going to take more than you think you can give, and then I'm going to take some more."

"Yes, please."

Simon spit into his hand and reached between them, his big hand encircling both of them. He gave a squeeze and the friction and the heat drove Adam into a frenzy. Adam tried to push into Simon's palm, tried to piston his bucking hips so he could come, but Simon was stronger and used his body weight to hold him still. To drive him insane.

They were lined up against each other perfectly and he wanted to see, wanted to watch, but he was pinned to the mattress and all he could do was accept the perfect pleasure Simon was forcing on him.

God, nothing had ever felt better than this big lumberjack pressing against him everywhere.

Simon's brawny frame, so massive and perfect, was better than any fantasy Adam had ever dreamed up. Adam slid his hand to Simon's ass and enjoyed feeling the big man shudder with barely contained pleasure. He wanted him lose control, to unleash all the power.

The delicious hard, sticky slide of their cocks was going to undo him, though. Too soon. He wanted Simon's mouth, he wanted Simon inside him, he wanted it all but Adam wasn't going to be able to hold out. Fireworks began exploding behind his eyes and they didn't stop over the next few hours as each thrill led to the next until they were boneless and satiated with pleasure and unable to do anything but sleep wrapped in each other's arms.

It had been a mistake.

One of his favorites, to be sure. But a mistake just the same.

Simon listened to Adam breathing and checked the urge to pull him closer. To revel in that body that seemed to have been made just for him.

But Simon wasn't ready for more than what they shared, and Adam had made it clear that he was. Even if he hadn't said it out loud. Adam deserved to find what he was looking for. Someone to be his partner in everything. God, he could say it now...a husband.

Simon had never given any thought to marriage when Michael was still alive. It had seemed as idealistic as winning the lottery someday. And after Michael died, he hadn't give relationships any thought at all.

But he bet Adam did. Adam was the kind of guy who would be good at being married. At sharing a life. He was also the kind of person who took care of people. The last thing Adam needed was to get caught up in trying to care about Simon. He'd waste a lot of time and effort and get nothing in return.

It would be better end this now before Adam got invested in trying to save Simon.

But god. Making love to the man had been a revelation. Adam was so expressive, so open and uninhibited. Simon had never been with someone who found so much joy in sex. He'd never laughed in bed. Never gone from tender to primal and back again so quickly. Sex in this century had been about a biological need for Simon. Sex with Adam had been about connecting to another person on every level.

And that was exactly why it wouldn't happen again.

Simon shouldn't have let it happen to begin with. When he'd come in from chopping wood yesterday, he'd thought he'd taken care of all the lingering sexual tension between he and Adam or he would have stayed out longer. But then Adam started with the buttons on Simon's shirt and the switch was flipped. Simon never needed anything, anyone, so desperately. There had been no more fight left in him. His only goal in life had been to get that man under him. Over him. Next to him. Hell, it hadn't mattered.

And thinking about it was steering Simon down the wrong path again. He needed to get outside. To be in the woods where he could think and breathe.

He slid out of bed and dressed in the dark. He'd leave a note in the kitchen. He didn't want to wake Adam or be there when Adam woke up full of Christmas and hope.

Chapter Six

Road is clear. Getting your car out of the ditch so you can be on your way today.

WELL, MERRY FUCKING CHRISTMAS TO you too, Simon.

It didn't take a genius to figure out what that note meant. Thanks for the sex. Go away now.

Adam supposed it wasn't a surprise, but he'd admit to not preparing himself for it very well. It hurt, dammit.

Adam knew he wasn't going to be Simon's endgame. But he figured they'd at least have Christmas. That they'd part amicably with memories of the few days they stepped out of time.

Simon was an asshole, but that didn't stop Adam from wanting him. It probably made him want him more. That was the funny thing about people, the way they could make you want them by pushing you away. Simon was not good for Adam. Adam knew that. He knew that Simon would be detrimental to Adam's hard earned self-respect, to his goals of finding a real partner. Of maybe starting a family.

But knowing that didn't make him less desirable. Knowing that if Simon just let himself, he could be kind of man Adam needed. Because Adam knew that he was already the kind of man that Simon needed.

When Simon came in from the snow, Adam was ready. He'd dressed in his *fancy* library clothes and he'd put on the face of the guy he'd practiced being a lot while navigating the singles scene of his old life. Sex was sex. Cock was cock. It wasn't about love. It was about the game. He got what he wanted. A good lay. A great night's sleep.

Silver Pines was a small town, but Simon the Recluse wouldn't be hard to avoid.

Simon glowered. As usual. "I'll drive you to your car." Not hello. Not Merry Christmas. Not good morning or how did you sleep or do you want to suck me off one more time before you go?

Shields up. "I can walk."

"I said I'll drive you."

He didn't want to argue, so went out to the truck. The ride was short in time, but long of things unsaid.

It wasn't until they pulled in behind his car that Adam spoke. "Thank you for getting my car unstuck." He wouldn't thank him for the hospitality. It would sound too much like he was thanking him for sex.

Simon blew out a breath. "I've never told anyone else about Michael. About the war."

Trust Simon to screw up the distant, polite, near stranger vibe he was going for. The man had literally no viable social skills.

Adam didn't want to open back up, but he remembered the man on the couch from last night, not the one writing a note this morning. "Thank you for telling me. It means a lot that you trusted me."

Simon blew out a breath. "You're too polite," he practically yelled. "I was a total asshole. You should stand up for yourself. Tell me off."

"So you can punish yourself for more? No thanks, I'd rather not be a part of your self-flagellation."

Simon grunted. "Merry Christmas."

He didn't know what to say to that. It could have been a merry one. It could have been the best day of his life. But that was just a dream. Resigned, Adam didn't respond and unbuckled his seatbelt. He was used to the hollow ache around his heart, but he didn't like it.

"Shit." Simon reached over and pulled him across the bench seat with one arm. Adam, off balance, used Simon's big body to steady himself on. Simon's features were pinched into anger, rage even. "I like being alone. I didn't ask for this," Simon said and then he punished Adam with a kiss.

There was no finesse, no exploring, Simon demanded with his fierce mouth and Adam angled his head to let him. The kiss wasn't about seduction, it was about distress. Simon's torment, Adam's frustration. The two tangled, dueling for a prize, for a win that wouldn't come. Because the more they kissed, the harder they pushed against each other, the more tormented and frustrated they became. The kiss was scorching hot and ice cold, and Simon broke off, thrusting Adam back from himself.

The windows fogged as their harsh breaths filled the cab. Adam reached over, but Simon withdrew further.

Hell.

"Merry Christmas, Simon." He got out and slammed the door. Wishing it would be that easy to slam the door on his feelings, but knowing he'd screwed up. Again. Wanting more than someone was willing, or able, to give. That was his specialty, wasn't it?

Chapter Seven

SIMON COULDN'T BEAR TO LOOK at the Christmas tree, so he sat in the kitchen area, turning his chair so he didn't have to see what he'd done.

He tried to remember that being a dick to Adam was for his own good. He tried to remember that it was too painful to love someone and lose him, it was better to not let anyone in. He couldn't hurt Adam and Adam couldn't hurt him.

Nobody could hurt Simon. Wasn't that right? Because Simon had given up on people the day Fracker chose death over his help. His touch.

Because he was polluted. Forsaken. Uninvited.

God, what if Michael had lived? Would they be together now? Still? He'd never questioned it before. His death had given the relationship martyr status. And had given Simon reason enough to never love again.

But Michael was just a man. Not an angel. He wouldn't have wanted to be Simon's forever-victim saint. His reason for living without life.

He thought of Fracker again. How he'd built up the last moments of the man's life into the avatar of Simon's future. But Fracker was also human. Sometimes he was an asshole. Most of the time he had been actually. And he might have come around, given time to deal with the shock that his brother had been lying to him. Of course, maybe he wouldn't have. But why did it matter so much to Simon?

Because Simon had been afraid that Fracker was right. And he'd spent the last decade and a half running from *himself*.

How stupid. How selfish.

Himself.

He looked at his hands. Scarred, beaten.

He looked around him, at the walls he'd hewn with those hands. The home he'd built.

The dog at his feet. The puppy in his lap.

He hadn't tainted them with his touch.

And his town? No matter how many times he said no, the people of Silver Pines invited him to every forsaken community dinner. To their homes. They pretended they didn't know he was the one who delivered free firewood to them when someone fell ill or lost a job. They never pushed him further than he'd allowed, but they didn't recoil from him either.

He thought of Stella—quirky Stella whom he could never tell no. She didn't suffer for knowing him, did she? She smiled happily, teased him. Made him feel like an irritable older brother. He hadn't ruined her by being in her proximity. If he looked into his heart, he loved her. Why had he put so many walls around their friendship?

One more look at his hands reminded him of what they'd looked like cupping Adam's face before he'd kissed him. What they looked like skimming the sinewy lines of Adam's body. What they'd felt like twisted in his hair.

God. He was an idiot.

He could have had all that life has to offer and instead he'd chosen to take only what barely sustained him.

He crossed the room to the telephone. His old rotary phone that worked when internet lines didn't.

Then he cursed and walked back away from it.

He was a coward.

No, no he wasn't. It was Christmas. If he believed in anything at all, today was the day it could happen.

He hadn't always been an ogre. Somewhere, very deep inside, the old Simon still lived and breathed. Every stupid Christmas movie he'd ever seen suddenly made sense. The magic was real.

Just yesterday, he'd been trying to avoid being a cliché. Today, he was going to be the biggest fucking Christmas Miracle Cliché he could manage. The Grinch, Scrooge—they had nothing on him.

He stalked back to the phone and dialed.

"Hello?"

"I need you."

Chapter Eight

"SIMON? IS THAT YOU?" STELLA asked. He could hear the surprise in her tone.

"Remember all the times you said 'I owe you one?'"

"Merry Christmas to you, too. Wait...is it Bingo? Is there something wrong?"

He glanced at the pup gnawing on patient Maya's foot. "No, he's fine." He paused. "But I'm not."

"Simon? What's wrong?" The concern in her voice overwhelmed him a little.

"I screwed up."

"Okay. Are you in jail?"

"No."

"Good. Because I maxed out my credit card Christmas shopping, and I was trying to figure out how I was going to raise bail."

"You'd bail me out of jail?"

"Of course. Now what do you need? And take your time telling me because otherwise I have to go back into the kitchen and help cook dinner and my sister is driving me insane with all her wedding nonsense."

"I hurt someone's feelings."

Silence.

"I don't know what to do about it."

"Simon, you're an ogre. What do you care if you hurt someone's feelings?" She was teasing, but it hit home.

He needed to change. And that wasn't going to happen by protecting himself anymore. He needed to fillet himself open and he might as well start with Stella. "I hurt someone's feelings after we had sex and now I'm in the doghouse. I should probably not do anything at all and let him be pissed at me so he moves on quickly. But I'm selfish and I don't want him to move on. I want to *un*hurt his feelings. How do I do that?"

"Are you drunk?"

"What? No. Are you going to help me or not?"

"Yes, of course I will. First of all, did you apologize? Because that's probably the first step to 'unhurt' his feelings."

"I need something bigger than that."

"So you are asking me to help you stage a grand gesture?" Her voice got that super peppy tone that usually meant trouble. Stella liked staging things.

A nasty thought occurred to him, poking a hole in his ballooning heart. "Hey. All these years, you've been throwing single men at me. Why didn't you try to connive me into a date with Adam?"

"The new librarian?" she asked.

"Yes. The new librarian. The single *gay* librarian who just moved to town. That guy. Do you think I'm not...?" Was he not good enough?

"Oh, Simon. I only threw guys at you when you weren't trying on your own. Every time I've seen you lately, you've been on your way to or from the library. It wasn't a stretch that you were already throwing yourself at him. Wait...is that whose feelings you hurt?"

"Help me, Stella."

"Oh, this is delicious."

Silence.

"Of course I will."

Adam was taking a pity-himself nap when the doorbell rang. Disoriented, he blinked, trying to remember what time of day it was.

He stumbled across the floor, thanks to the afghan wrapped around his legs, but when he opened it, he thought maybe he was still dreaming.

"Stella?"

She smiled brightly.

"Why are you wearing a top hat? And a tuxedo?"

"It's a super long story and I'll tell you while you change clothes."

She was always a little off. "Why am I changing clothes?"

"Do you trust me?"

He shook his head. "Not really."

She gave him "bitch, please" face and he opened the door wider to let her in.

"What should I be changing into?"

"Jeans and this." She handed him a bag.

"Can I ask why?"

She shook her head. "It's Christmas. The season of doing what crazy townspeople tell you to do."

"Right." He opened the bag. Red, green, tinsel...he closed the bag. "No."

"It's a Christmas sweater."

"I can see that. No." He was not a fan of Christmas this year. Also, no self-respecting gay dude would wear what was in that bag.

"Look. I know you don't know me very well. And that this is all very strange. But believe me when I tell you that you absolutely want to put that sweater on and come with me. It will be the thing you will be grateful for even thirty years from now."

She looked so earnest. And a little crazy-eyed. But he obviously didn't have anything better to do. So he put the sweater on and then followed her out to the street.

THE CHRISTMAS CONTRADICTION

Where a horse and buggy awaited, festooned with garland and red bows.

He paused and found Stella's over-eager face smiling at him. He had a sinking feeling in his stomach. She had to know he was gay, right? It wasn't a secret. She seemed like a nice girl, but he wasn't interested in trying out for other team just because—

"Merry Christmas, Adam."

He turned back to the buggy. Back to the deep voice. Simon stood next to the steps. He looked so good wrapped in a black coat and red scarf.

"Simon, what is going on here?"

"Talk in the buggy," Stella said, ushering him towards Simon.

He didn't want to.

He wanted to more than anything.

Then he saw that Maya and Bingo were on the bench seat and he couldn't resist figuring out where this would take him. He climbed in, aware Simon was watching his ass as he did. When Simon took a seat next to him, Adam tried breathing through his nose so he wouldn't be brought under by the scent that made him ache.

"I'm not sure what's going on. But I'm still pissed at you," Adam said baldly. Because he needed to remind himself.

"I know."

Stella was their driver, apparently. And she got the carriage moving through the perfect town square. Christmas music poured from the little CD player in front of them.

The power had never gone out in town, and all the white lights and snow made it look like a picture perfect postcard. He held on to his anger, barely. The people who lived right in town were on their porches waving to them. He looked at Simon again, confused that he didn't seem surprised or all that bothered by it. Even stranger, people filled in the street behind them. Like they were some kind of parade.

"What the hell is going on?"

Simon turned to him. "You were right. About me. About a lot of things. I wanted to apologize for the way I treated you, but it didn't seem like that was enough. I'm out of practice at this kind of thing."

Well, that felt good. But didn't explain everything. "Why am I wearing a Christmas sweater?"

Simon opened his coat to reveal a matching atrocity. "You were missing out on a boisterous family and 109 snow globes, so we decided to make it up to you."

Still shocked at seeing Simon wearing a Santa sweater, he asked, "We?"

"Stella's interpretation of grand gesture and mine might be a little different. I have a feeling this is going to get worse."

They finally stopped in front of the community hall. Half the town ushered them into the old building all lit up, glowing actually. Inside, it appeared that everyone had packed up their Christmas dinners and brought them in potluck style. Kids were running around, Santa was sitting in a chair, there were decorations everywhere and none of them matched. Simon led him to one side of the room where tables had been pushed against the wall. On top of the tables, snow globes in all shapes and sizes.

"Simon?"

"I asked everyone who had them to bring them in. There are 279. We beat your aunt."

Adam couldn't believe it. "This is...breathtaking and a little weird."

Strong arms turned him away from the table. "I'm sorry. I wish I had treated you better. You made me feel alive for the first time in over a decade and I made you feel bad instead. And I'm sorry."

"You did all of this for me?" Adam asked, his voice cracking as the rest of the room fell away and there was only the two of them. The librarian and the lumberjack.

"Stella arranged most of it." Simon swallowed hard. "I'm rusty at this kind of thing."

"You're standing here in a room full of Christmas cheer, wearing an ugly sweater, and telling me about your feelings. Who are you?"

"Do you like it?"

"It's awful. I love it."

Simon stole a glance at the room and growled quietly. "You know they are all staring at us right now."

"Yeah. I...apology accepted?" Because what else could Adam do? Simon surprised him, and while Adam was tempted to protect his heart, he didn't have the strength to. Not when Simon had put himself out there so far, so publicly.

He'd thought a lot about Simon's story about the asshole Fracker and Simon's boyfriend, Michael. Losing his love would have been devastating enough, but also to lose his self-identity, to be turned away by someone he probably had considered closer than a brother. It wasn't hard to see why a man would shut down.

But he wasn't shut down now. He was smiling and looking uncomfortable and probably wished he was anywhere but in the middle of the entire town at a Christmas party trying to apologize to Adam. But there he was anyway.

And then Simon's expression changed from hopeful to wolfish. Exactly the way Adam liked him best.

"You should probably get something to eat." Simon leaned down, speaking directly into his ear. "When I get you back to my house, into my bed, I'm going to tear that ugly Santa sweater off your gorgeous body and do everything you ever dreamed of."

Chapter Nine

THE IMPROMPTU CHRISTMAS PARTY HADN'T lasted long. People seemed to understand that Simon was going to need an adjustment period, even if he had jumped all in to the festivities.

Or maybe they just wanted to go back home to their own, planned Christmases.

After stopping at Adam's apartment, where it went unspoken that he was just there to grab a bag, they drove back to Simon's cabin.

His librarian had grown introspective over the last twenty minutes. "You're quiet," Simon said.

"Thinking."

"About?"

Adam turned to him. "You want to know what I'm thinking?"

"Always."

"I can accept Christmas miracles occur. But what prompted this one? When you left me—"

"You prompted the miracle, Adam." Adam slid his hand over and Simon grasped it. "You were right about me living in the past. It was like that one day of my life was my touchstone. Everything I thought and felt always went back to the four hours of my life when I learned my lover died and my brother rejected me." Simon didn't know if he could say it all right. That's why he'd wanted Stella's help. But it was all on him now. "I don't want to be alone, but what killed me was knowing that I'd made you feel lonely. I don't ever want to be the reason you hurt again."

God. What if he was overdoing this?

"What do you want, though, Adam?" Because he supposed he'd better ask. It was possible that Adam was just trying to be nice and going along with a pretty crazy turn of events.

"I want you, Simon. Whatever and however much of you I can get."

Simon pulled into his long driveway, replaying the first time Adam had said those words to him. Was it only last night? How could he have lived so much more in twenty-four hours than he had in thirteen years? "I don't want you to feel pressured. Christmas, a small town full of busybodies, a beast kidnapping you to his lair again."

"I'm where I want to be."

Simon was suddenly very nervous. What if he screwed this up? What if tomorrow he woke up and his heart went back to three times smaller? What if Adam realized he needed a man with more finesse, without so much baggage?

"Jesus, Simon. Relax."

He realized his agitation had caused him to squeeze Adam's hand. "Sorry. Not good at this."

"I recall you're very good at the next part, so let's just focus on that for now. We're almost home and this sweater is itching to come off. Literally. Itching."

Home. He'd said home. Simon parked the truck and snow began to fall. He hoped the power went out again. He hoped he got snowbound with his sexy librarian for days, weeks.

They made it into the house, settled the dogs, stoked the fire, and then he began to strip Adam of all this Christmas trimmings.

He wanted to tell him that he loved him, but it was too soon. Instead he showed him. Several times.

Chapter Ten

Two months later

THE LIBRARY DOOR OPENED WITH a *whoosh* of wind behind it. Adam could tell by the stomp of boots which patron it was that entered. He rolled his eyes. Something had disturbed the bear again.

He rounded the stacks to find a hulking beast pacing in front of the checkout desk.

"Mr. Powell, are you here about your library fines?"

Simon whirled around, and Adam didn't know how it was that he didn't tip right over. He was so big, so burly. *So mine.*

"A goat," he said.

What? "No, I won't take a goat. You owe $8.10."

Simon shook his head. "Stella is trying to make me take a goat. What am I going to do with a goat?"

"Feed it, I guess."

Simon let out a sturdy sigh. "Why does she give me all her misfits?"

"Because you are a big softie?"

"That's not what you said last night."

Adam brushed by him, barely touching him, but enough that he knew Simon was hooked. And watching his ass.

Simon smiled and Adam's gut clenched. Wow. He was never prepared for the rare sighting.

"If you lock those doors, librarian, I'll give you a down payment on those fines right now."

Oh, if only. "I don't think so. Much as I'd like to take you up on that, it's moving day, remember? I have to turn in my key at six and I still have one more load."

"No you don't. I brought the rest of the boxes home this afternoon. You're officially living with me now, roomie."

Adam swallowed down the lump in his throat. Maybe they were moving too fast. But he hadn't been to his apartment in weeks. "I hope you're sure about this, Simon. The roof leak in the building will be fixed as soon as the weather clears. I didn't have to move out permanently."

"Me sure?" He cupped Adam's jaw. "I asked you to move in on Christmas."

"You've lived alone for a long time. This is a big change."

"I don't want to wake up in a bed you're not in."

Adam smiled. He wished he could go back in time and tell his teen self that everything will work out okay. That kid, young Adam, had been too thin, too gangly. His glasses always smudged. He'd liked the wrong things—books not sports, boys not girls. He'd thought being introverted was a curse. Now, Adam stood, surrounded by books, wanted by a man who treated his glasses like they were the most precious thing in the world, who worshiped his body every night, and was more introverted than even Adam. But being introverted with your favorite person in the world wasn't such a bad thing.

Simon stroked his thumb across Adam's jaw, bringing him back to the present. "Where did you just go, librarian?"

Adam kissed the inside of Simon's wrist. "Memory Lane. I'll lock up and we can go home." He moved to the desk to grab his jacket.

"Adam?"

"Yeah?" He turned, his breath catching like it always did when his strapping boyfriend looked at him like that. Like he was one part feral beast and one part a man head over heels.

"I was going to give you a key to the cabin, but since I don't lock the door it seemed silly. But I want this to mean something. You moving in."

"It means something." But Simon looked suddenly greenish gray. "You okay?"

"No. I can't hear anything over the roar in my ears." Simon swallowed hard. "I knew I'd mess this up."

"Mess what up? What is wrong?"

"I haven't said the words. And you deserve the words." Simon's color returned and he took a deep breath, taking a few steps closer to Adam while he pulled something from his pocket.

The words. Quickly, Adam took an inventory of everything around him so he would always remember this moment. The smell of the books and Simon's soap. The late afternoon light filtering through the windows. The silence of the stacks and the thumping of his heart.

Simon cleared his throat. "I was going to wait until we were home, but I'll have a stroke if I try to put it off any longer." Simon took Adam's hand into his meaty paws. "I thought I had forgotten how to love. But you remind me how every day. I love you."

He would not cry. He would not cry. He would not...Adam's throat tightened. "I love you, too."

"I'm not a rich man." He held one hand up so Adam wouldn't interrupt him. "My life is comfortable, but it will never be grand. I have a feeling you moved here because money isn't that important to you, and I know you've been happy the last two months. Happy with me. With our home. But it's important to me that you know I will always provide for you. Whatever you need. And before you go off all half-cocked, I know you make your own money and your own way. It's just that the easiest way I know how to show you I love you is to take care of you and let you take care of me. And you do." He opened Adam's hand and placed a ring in his palm. "I'm not getting on a knee or you'd have to pull me up after. But this ring belonged to my dad. I asked my mom to send it to me two weeks ago. When you're ready, I'd like you to put it on."

Wow. Adam looked at the ring. He'd been expecting an "I love you" not an engagement ring.

"I don't know what to say," he began.

"Don't say anything now. I waited a long time to find you. I'll wait however long you need."

Adam clenched his fingers around the ring. "So you don't want me to tell you yes right now?"

Simon grunted. "I put you on the spot. Don't feel pressured—"

Adam barreled into Simon and kissed him hard. "Yes, Simon. Yes I love you." Kiss. "Yes I want to live with you in a cabin in the woods." Kiss. "Yes I want to be your husband." Kiss. "Yes I want to take care of you and let you take care of me." Kiss. "And yes, I will pay your library fees from our joint account when we first open one." Kiss.

They kissed at the door. They kissed in the truck. And they almost got all the way home when they remembered they had to turn around and pick up Stella's goat.

Dear Reader,

I hope you enjoyed the charming coastal town of Silver Pines, WA. Nestled between the Strait of Juan de Fuca and the Olympic Mountains, Silver Pines is known for clean air, majestic views, heartwarming, sexy romance, and more than its fair share of shenanigans. Don't want to miss the next book? Sign up for my spam free mailing list.

<u>Newsletters are sexy!</u>

As always, leaving a review is much appreciated and I love hearing from readers. I'm pretty easy to find...@gwenhayes on Twitter or <u>gwen@gwenhayes.com</u>.

Until next time,

Gwen

Ours is Just a Little Sorrow

The colony of New Geneva has risen from the ashes of her dying mother planet, Earth, by rebuilding a society based on a time before everything went horribly, horribly wrong...the Victorian Era...

Violet Merriweather first sets eyes on Colonel Winston when he purchases her at auction from Witherspoon Academy, the orphanage where she'd been raised after her rescue from Earth. Dutifully, as she was taught, Violet pushes away her fear of the monstrous, forbidding Thornfield Abbey, and throws herself into her work as governess to the Colonel's youngest son.

But the Colonel's elder sons have other ideas.

John and Gideon Winston are as different as night and day, and each wants to claim Violet for his own. John immediately charms her with his intelligence and cordial demeanor, while Gideon, the dark rogue, delights in flustering her at every opportunity, awakening a yearning she doesn't understand and most assuredly does not want. She tries to deny her pull to both men, but an uneasy midnight bargain with one forges a new alliance as she's dazzled by an underground New Geneva she hadn't known existed. And temptations she cannot resist.

But something is preying on the women of New Geneva, something that threatens to unleash the ghosts of Thornfield and drag them all into hell. And that something wants Violet most of all.

Ours is Just a Little Sorrow by Gwen Hayes

Chapter One

THE FIRST TIME I ever laid eyes on Colonel Malcolm Winston, he was purchasing me at a private sale arranged for his convenience.

The brass of his buttons shone like stars against the navy of his uniform as he pointed his walking stick at me lazily, as if he were already bored with the duty. A sneering bulldog carved from ivory, or perhaps bone, topped the cane. The Colonel shook it a little harder at me, in another impatient gesture, when nobody made a move quick enough to his liking.

Mrs. Witherspoon inclined her head in acquiescence and gestured me back into the line with her sharp gaze. I jerked into place beside the others. The blood rushed to my cheeks in a hot wave, and then absented them just as quickly, leaving me weak from its sudden change of course. Why had he chosen me? All five of us were outfitted in the same dark gray gowns. Our hair done in the same practical shape. Our boots all the same shabby, well-worn leather. What had set me apart from the other four?

"She'll do," he said gruffly.

I didn't raise my eyes to his again, but I could feel his scrutinizing gaze on me as if he were touching me with embers from a fire. Instead, I stared at the scuffed planks of the floor.

My life would forever change because I would do.

My valise was already packed when I returned to our sleeping quarters. It hadn't been my valise an hour ago, of course, as I never had reason to pack my meager belongings before. I hadn't slept a night away from Witherspoon Academy of Fine Ladies of Suitable Nature since I'd been brought there at the age of six. I had no family, save my academy sisters, and I was loath to leave them, even the bratty ones. I always knew this day would come, and yet somehow, I felt so unprepared for it.

The dormitory already seemed like a memory, even as I stood in it. Nothing in the room had changed in twelve years, save the girls that came and went. The beds lined one long wall, serviceable and plain, yet always comfortable and clean. The academy had been a haven, even if it had been an oppressive one.

Shelby, my dearest friend, sent me a watery smile as we found my bag far more ready to leave than I was. Bless her. I would miss that face and those round spectacles. Shelby was my age, according to the records, but she always seemed younger. Perhaps it was the reluctance of the baby fat to leave her cheeks, but I suspected it was the childlike innocence that clung to her despite the harsh lot she'd been given.

"I suppose the Colonel is waiting," Shelby said. Alongside the tremor, there was a hint of something else in her voice. Wonderment maybe. It must have occurred to her that it might have just as easily been her leaving this time.

I nodded and reached for one last hug. "I won't forget you, Shelby. If given the occasion to, I will write you as often as I can."

"Oh, Violet," she cried. She squeezed hard, threatening injury to my ribs. As we pulled away from the embrace, Penelope slid around the corner through the doorway, breathless and sweating.

"A governess," she blurted on a loud exhale from her exertion. "I found the file on Witherspoon's PEAD. The Colonel is here only for a governess."

"Oh, thank God," Shelby said, dangerously close to swooning.

I didn't want to know how Penelope had once again cracked the password on Mrs. Witherspoon's Personal Engine Analytical Device; I was just so very glad she'd been able to. Penny had never met a difference engine she couldn't hack. A hazardous and unseemly talent, and yet one that had benefited me more than once.

A governess. That I could do. Relief claimed my lungs, forcing out a sigh.

Witherspoon's Academy of Fine Ladies of Suitable Nature had always been intended to provide its clients with exemplary governesses or ladies' companions. The last two of our sisters, however, were sold as brides. We'd been trained for that, too, of course. The thought was daunting just the same. Mrs. Witherspoon hadn't been happy about it, but the market had dictated that she often make difficult choices.

While nobody especially liked Mrs. Witherspoon and her pinched expressions, we all respected her. She never put what was best for one above what was best for the school. I'd never been asked to make a sacrifice that didn't benefit all my sisters, the current and future ones.

And because of Mrs. Witherspoon's hard decisions, I was about to embark on a life far different than the one I'd have had without the help of the good citizens of New Geneva. The children of my own planet, Earth, fought hard to chisel a life that ended at an average age of five and twenty. Their existence was one of hunger and violence, while I had grown up with a full belly and clean sheets.

And now, I was to make my way in the world armed with an education of quality, an education that was not only of books, but lessons in practicality as well. I owed the irritable Mrs. Witherspoon, whose lack of husband made the "Mrs." part of her name dubious at best, more than I could ever repay.

The girls lined the hall outside the dormitory for farewells. Shelby did not join them; our goodbye was private and tearful. My duty to my other sisters was quite different. I was already changed. No longer one of them, I needed to project an attitude of a calm lady, not an emotional schoolgirl. It was for them that I soldiered my spine and remained polite, but slightly aloof, as I bid them farewell one last time. I did not want to leave them worried or anxious of their own future, though I was terrified of my own.

At the end of the line, Mrs. Witherspoon looked down her hawk nose at me for a long moment. In her gaze, I glimpsed the woman, not the headmistress, and I was grateful for the short connection.

She nodded briskly. "Very well, Miss Merriweather."

And that was that.

Mrs. Witherspoon accompanied me to the door. Outside a pneumatic hover taxi waited. I was surprised, as I had expected the Colonel would have saved the money and ensconced me in the coach with him. It seemed an extravagant waste to send two carriages to one address. Perhaps he thought I needed a little time alone to acclimate myself to my new life and position. Maybe he had no interest in being cooped up with me for the long trip. Likelier, he felt I wasn't important enough to ride in his own coach.

It mattered not. I chose to be grateful for the time alone. There was never much opportunity to be singularly alone at the academy. Often, I would stay awake long into the night just to hear myself think.

The coachman barely waited for me to buckle my harness before we were in motion. Even at the speed that I'm sure at times doubled the legal limit, it still took more than an hour to reach our destination. As we climbed altitude, higher and higher, there were fewer and fewer signs of civilization. In the middle of nothing it seemed, the coachman stopped the vehicle at a black iron gate almost hidden in the brush. We sat motionless while a robotical avian left its perch on one of the spires and flew around the taxi, stopping like a hummingbird in front of each window. Its copper "feathers" made a tiny mechanical grinding noise as it flapped its wings. Its beady red eyes relayed our electromagnetic optical images to someone on the other side of the gate who would decide whether or not we were welcome.

I half-hoped we were not.

As soon as the thought crossed my mind, I discounted it and chided myself. How foolish to be put off my future by a flying automaton. Just the same, I didn't like its red-devil eyes.

The gate opened slowly to a forest. A rather dense forest. The coachman groaned at the sight of the very narrow and twisting path before us. The further we ventured, the fewer the aether gaslamps became, and the darker our environment grew. As we had to travel at reduced speed to stay on the path, I had more opportunity than I wished for to watch my surroundings. The trees held secrets and they whispered to each other in the rustling of leaves. The avian automaton followed us as if we were being herded. I wondered if it had other uses, besides spying. Perhaps it was also a weapon to be used against those who didn't wish to be herded. I imagined sharp lightning bolts striking me from those horrible red eyes.

At last we came to a clearing, and there, obstructing views to all else, loomed an imposing castle with angry turrets poking the sky. There were too many raw angles and too much rock. It seemed like teeth of a huge creature more than a home. My new home, it would seem.

As the coachman help me to the ground, a bitter wind kicked up a prickling message of warning wherever it touched my skin. I shivered, but thrust out my chin with fortitude and marched up the steps. I would not be deterred by childish fears. The wind could not hurt me unless I chose to let it signify something nefarious.

A tall, lanky servant opened the door and directed a footman to retrieve my valise from the coachman. The butler, I assumed, introduced himself as Oliver and showed me to a salon where I might take refreshment whilst I waited. Waited for what, I didn't know, for Oliver was less than communicative. He walked slowly, his droopy Basset hound eyes staring straight ahead. I believed he was the most depressed person I had ever met, and I grew up in an orphanage.

Despite the serious nature of the castle's exterior and its butler, the salon was welcoming. Though heavy drapes were pulled against the sun, many lamps burned from wall sconces and table tops, corded by tubes glowing with liquideous aether. The clean scent of lemons fragranced the air, a testament to the highly polished gleam of every surface. On the mantel, several framed lithographs changed their image on a loop. Mesmerized, I watched the ancestors of the Colonel flash by, one after the other.

"If you happen across one with two young boys baring their bottoms at the lake, I can assure you I will never tell you which bottom belongs to me."

At the sound of the male voice, I turned abruptly towards the door.

The young man was, perhaps, five years my senior, dressed impeccably, and smiling at me with a slightly incorrigible, but mostly pleasant fashion. He bowed politely, and I returned with an automatic curtsy. As he continued his entrance into the room, his smile grew warmer, as did my cheeks. Good heavens, he was quite the figure of a man.

"Aren't you going to ask?" he wondered.

"Ask what, sir?"

"Which bottom belongs to me?"

I am sure my face matched the red velvet drapery, but as was my way, I didn't let embarrassment hinder forward progress. "Unfortunately, good sir, I hadn't had the fortune of coming upon that particular image as of yet."

He stopped right in front of me. His eyes were a beautiful shade of blue, like the skies on a cloudless day. "Welcome to Thornfield Abbey. Are you the new governess, then?"

I curtsied again. "Violet Merriweather. I am pleased to make your acquaintance."

"I'm John Winston, the Colonel's son." He smiled again, his face obviously used to the action, so unlike his father's.

Goodness. My heart pattered much too hard. Were I given to swooning and fainting, I should have required salts. Instead, I returned his easy smile. "Surely, you are not my new charge?"

John Winston barked with an unexpected laugh. "Alas, no. It is my younger brother in need of chaperonage."

Another voice joined us then. A deeper, richer voice, laced with a sardonic quality I didn't believe John could possess. "Indeed, that I am."

Leaning against the jamb, a young man leered at us before he drank from the amber liquid in his glass. From across the room, it was apparent that his clothes were quality, like John's, but the stranger wore them with a disheveled grace. His white shirt was not fastened all the way, exposing far more of his throat than was proper. His jacket was slung over his arm, and a cravat hung loose and undone around his neck. His hair, darker than midnight, was shrubbed about as if he'd recently left his pillow.

He straightened and bowed like John had, only it seemed the opposite of courteous. His eyes held mine in challenge as he inclined his head and body, and as my body responded in a curtsey by habit, I somehow felt judged for it being so rote. As if my well-practiced manners were an affront to him.

"Miss Merriweather," John said tightly. "May I present to you my younger brother, Gideon Winston, as he darkens the door way." John seemed resigned, as if an introduction were a bad idea. "Gideon, this is Violet Merriweather, the new governess."

Gideon crossed the room in a graceful gliding fashion, and I imagined suddenly that he would be a wonderful dancer. He reached for my hand and kissed the inside my wrist just above the line of my glove while he stared into my eyes like he was daring me.

My pulse skittered madly from the shock of his lips on my bare skin. I wished for the first time that I were the swooning type, anything to end this wild moment that seemed to stretch longer and longer, pulling me into an abyss of feeling I didn't understand. His eyes were blue also, but not like the day lit skies of John's eyes, rather the color of the ocean at storm. And that storm was thrashing me about, pushing me under the waves of Gideon's making. He seemed to understand his power over me, for at that moment he winked and dropped my hand as if it had never happened.

"Certainly you are not my charge either," I stammered, resisting the urge to rub my still tingling wrist.

"No, Miss Merriweather," John said, his voice like a life preserver in the tumultuous seas I'd been treading. I clung to the rope of his words and let him reel me back to safety. "Though Gideon could use a chaperone more than anyone I know, it is our youngest brother, Phillip, who will require your services. He's to turn five next month."

Briskly nodding, my pulse slowed and my breath returned to a natural cadence. I stood like the tip of a triangle between the two brothers, each so different from each other, and though I was reluctant to believe in such things, a sense of foreboding settled into my bones as they looked first at each other and then to me. I should not like to find myself in this geometric position, but I felt hopeless to stop what seemed so inevitable. It was as if we were all aware that our future was being written in that moment, and we were all powerless to fight the furious quill.

Chapter Two

AS IF SENT from God or the devil himself to break the tension filled moment I was sharing with the brothers Winston, a whirling dervish of what I assumed was young master Phillip, spun through the room chasing an aero-winged flyer that had gotten free from his control.

"Ho there!" John cried as he ducked just in time to avoid serious head injury. "I say, Phillip, turn that thing off."

"It won't listen," Phillip complained, holding aloft the metal box of gears that should have controlled the flight.

John raced to the flyer while Gideon beckoned me to join him as he dashed to the pianoforte. He pushed me under first and then took shelter next to me. We watched the show while John tried to catch the aeroship. He tagged it once with an athletic jump into the air, but the toy eluded his grasp while maintaining a now dodgier flight owing to its bent wing.

The aeroship turned on Phillip then, so I waved him to our hiding spot. It chased him all the way to the pianoforte, until he dove into our nook. Gideon snatched the box from him while I tucked the young boy into my side protectively.

"Who are you?" he asked.

I looked into his sweet face and fell into instant adoration. He had Gideon's eyes and dark hair, but his quick toothless grin reminded me instantly of John. The brothers Winston definitely knew how to entangle a girl quickly.

"I am your new governess, Phillip. You may call me Miss Merriweather in the company of others, but you will likely call me a bitter, hissing crone when you are alone for I intend to make you study very hard and become a great man."

The aeroship whizzed by us once more, making a sick choking sound.

Phillip smiled at me. "I don't like reading, but maths and art ain't so bad."

"They aren't so bad," I corrected.

At that moment, the flying toy crashed into a display of vases just as a voice boomed from the doorway. "What is the damned ruckus?"

Phillip shrank into my side a little deeper while John explained to the Colonel the happenstance we'd found ourselves, pausing while he trapped the ship against the wall. The Colonel glared in turn at each of us. It perhaps wasn't the best first impression of a governess to find her crouching under one's pianoforte, but then again, it could be said that it was his own fault for not interviewing me properly.

Not that I had any intention of telling him that.

The Colonel's face was mottled red and he seethed unhappily while John took apart the toy with a tool he had in his pocket. I wondered why he carried such a tool with him, whether this kind of occurrence was, perhaps, not unusual.

To my relief, the Colonel left the room, containing his rage to one slam of the door. The ornate tick-tocker on the wall began to play its chimes to signify it was tea time. I crawled from my spot, dismayed that not one of the Winstons offered me assistance. I sat on my knees and looked over my shoulder to Phillip.

"Phillip, when you find yourself hiding under a pianoforte with a lady, it is customary to stand first and then offer a hand to help her rise."

While Phillip scrambled from the nook to do his duty, Gideon smirked at me. "Customary, you say, Miss Merriweather? Do ladies hide under pianofortes often then?"

I ignored his pithy remark and allowed young Phillip to be a gentleman, though I could have used a little more heft than he had to offer. John barely registered our movement, so intent on fiddling with the aeroship that I think he'd quite forgotten the rest of us were in the room.

Since there seemed to be no Mrs. Winston about, I rang for tea, pulling the long tasseled cord. I sat as if nothing were amiss, though I felt the pins sliding through my hair awkwardly releasing my twist. What a day I'd already had.

John absently took a seat, still distracted by the mechanisms of the broken toy. Like John, Gideon also took a seat, but unlike John, there was nothing absent about his motions. He was far too intense, I decided. The way he watched me waiting for tea made me nervous.

Luckily, the tray walked in, behaving much better than the errant aeroship. I'd never seen one so grand. We only had one very old tea automaton at the academy, and it wasn't for everyday use, but rather for practice. This trolley was free of encumbering rust and likely oiled every day. The two mechanical robot legs worked together between two in-line bicycle wheels, propelling the wheels to roll each time one automated foot touched the ground. It stopped in front of me, and I began the tea service as I'd been taught.

The tea table itself was built over the front wheel; over the back wheel was the food table. Below the heated plate for the tea and cooled plates for the refreshments, a series of tubes ran liquideous aether through small boilers and iced bricks. Plates of cakes, sandwiches, and a tea service set into molds sat atop the tray itself so as not to jostle free.

Phillip eyed the cakes with delirious fascination.

His nanny came in to collect him, apologizing for losing track of her charge and leaning heavily on a cane. She was old, far too old for such a daunting task as keeping an active boy like Phillip in line. I wondered why she hadn't retired decades ago, and why nobody had thought to replace her.

"I should like to take tea with Phillip every day, in order to teach him the manners in a parlor as part of his curriculum. Will that be a problem?" I asked.

She looked so relieved at the thought I thought she might lie down right there. "I'll make sure he's ready for you every day, Miss Merriweather."

She turned and trudged out, far less graceful than the automaton had breezed in. How odd that she continued to work so far into her elderly years.

"Phillip," I said, as I poured the tea. "Please tell me how many cakes there are on the plate."

He counted slowly, but correctly.

"Excellent." I began putting the cakes on plates. "If we each have one, how many will be left?"

"One?" He sighed. "I don't know if I can do many more numbers if don't get at least two. I'm tired, you see."

Precocious child. "If you tell me the correct answer, you may have two."

Phillip lit up and began the process of take away. The entire conversation was watched avidly by Gideon. Though I tried to put all my focus on Phillip, the awareness of his older brother's gaze never left me.

His eyes bore into me, trying to ferret out secrets. Odd that he should think I had any. "Have you any memories of Earth, Miss Merriweather?" he asked finally, after the awkward scrutiny had continued for far too long.

I raised the cup to my lips for an extra moment of thinking time before I answered. "None, sir," I lied easily. "I was near Master Phillip's age when I was rescued by the good people of New Geneva."

Gideon pulled a flask from the pocket of his discarded jacket. As he poured a nip into his teacup, he chuckled wryly. "Yes, the good people rescued you. How kind to save you in order that they might put you into service for them."

My proud chin often had a will of its own, and it stubbornly rose above our shared station. "I enjoy teaching children and am grateful for the opportunities my education has provided."

Gideon left off his tea altogether and nipped directly from his flask. "I meant no disrespect."

Somehow, his apology didn't sway my opinion of his rancor. I knew it wasn't my place to care, but something about his attitude goaded me into defensiveness. "Do you find that people in service are of less value somehow than those who...I'm sorry, what is it that you do, sir?" Since he'd obviously just returned home in mid-day from whatever nocturnal excursion he'd participated in the night before, I guessed he had no occupation other than being the son of a rich man.

"Touché, Miss Merriweather." He perused me with a glance from head to toe, and then settled back to my lips. "I think a better question might be, what is it I don't do?"

His attention to my lips caused them to dry like a grape in the sun. I wanted nothing more than to wet them with my tongue, but knew that would be a mistake. A grave one.

John cleared his throat. "Miss Merriweather, I'm certain that you're in need of a short rest from your long day. Oliver can show you to your room, if you like. I'll make certain that Phillip is returned to the nursery."

"Yes," Gideon drawled. "She's likely tired from being purchased. By all means, let's get her a nap."

The flush of my face went hot and then cold as I gasped. John growled Gideon's name lowly.

"What?" Gideon asked. "Are we not to talk about it, then? "

I interrupted Gideon. "Phillip, would you please find out if my accommodations are ready? Oliver, I believe, would know for certain."

As soon as he was out of hearing range, I pinned Gideon with my most indignant expression. "In a very short time, sir, I have come to understand your character and your apparent dissatisfaction with the society that enables you to live in this grand home. I urge you, however, to please have a care with young Phillip's impressionable age when you seek to disparage the very life I lead."

"My brother does not disparage you, Miss Merriweather, he saves that for his family. Nothing we do is quite up to his ideals." John's voice may have been full of acrimony, but it was underlined with a curious sadness that led me to believe he wished very much for a different relationship with his brother.

"Yes, my ideals. Those pesky ethics I seem to cart around like a heavy pack." Gideon pulled another healthy swig from his flask. "I'm so burdened by principles."

The weight of the air pressed on the three of us. "I'm not ashamed," I said finally.

"My father bought you!" Gideon ran a hand through his messy locks. "As if you were a vase or a turnip at the market."

My jaw felt as if I had an iron pipe holding it in place. "Your father repaid the investment society put into my education and upbringing. I am not a turnip." I said the words, but I felt as if I were once again standing in that line of girls, waiting to learn what we'd fetch for a price.

I met Gideon's eyes and suddenly felt even more vulnerable, as if I were standing in front of him naked. He stripped me of my pride in one afternoon, shunting aside all that I'd packed carefully into my head the years at the academy. He gave voice to the feelings I could ill afford. Gideon was far more dangerous than an asp. At least a snake didn't shred your esteem before it bit.

"Tell me why the good people of New Geneva cannot simply save the poor children of Earth without exacting a penance of servitude? Surely we have enough resources to accommodate those less fortunate than ourselves."

John had gone back to tinkering with the aeroship, leaving me to argue politics with Gideon. Were there any two less capable people to discuss current events than us? A governess with no rights, and a nihilist with all of them.

Though it would have been best for me to excuse myself from the conversation, I found myself replying, "Perhaps you should take a seat in legislation if you feel so strongly about the ills of society."

"Ho," he laughed. "That would indeed be something. I assure you, Miss Merriweather, if you ever pass me in the hall and I tell you I'm bound for Parliament, take cover immediately and make peace with your God, for the end is nigh."

"I'll keep that in mind, sir." I rose from my seat; the gentlemen also stood. "Thank you for the lovely tea. I'll take my leave now."

John bowed, but Gideon only arched his acrimonious eyebrow at me. I would need to steer clear of him as much as possible if I wanted to find any satisfaction in my new post. I doubted it would be difficult, as I didn't foresee him being even vaguely interested in early morning constitutionals or lessons with young Phillip. Still, if I were expected to dine with the adults in the evening, he was sure to sour my appetite.

Dear Shelby,

As promised, a missive to let you know I'm doing well. Very well, indeed. I hope you are remaining in fine health and spirits, also. My charge, the young Phillip Winston, is bright and receptive to learning. I feel very privileged to have found such a position. I'm writing to you from my very own PEAD, if you can imagine. It was in my quarters the second morning of my employment. I hope I never forget my password—Penelope is too far to crack it for me.

I think of you often, but most especially when I take my daily walk for I pass the stable and remember how much you adored horses. The Winstons have only one and it belongs to the middle son of Colonel Winston. He seems to have an affinity with animals that he doesn't share with humans.

Strike that. It was unkind of me to say such a thing.

Please write to me if you can. I continue to miss you and hope you are well.

Yours in Friendship,
Violet

Two weeks later, I was breakfasting with a silent Colonel, who also had a way of souring my appetite. I'm not sure why he chose to have me take my meals with the family. I'd have been content to dine with the servants, but my position seemed to uncomfortably hover somewhere between the two worlds.

The Colonel and Gideon had similar dispositions of disdain and rancor, only each seemed to hold the exact opposite opinion. Neither had much use for me, which was likely for the best. I didn't cower in the Colonel's presence, but I didn't seek out his attention either. Breakfast was generally a somber affair until John graced the table. He always knew how to cajole and amuse us both.

The Colonel's fist slammed the table as he read from his PEAD. "Damned rebels!"

"Colonel?" I inquired.

"Scallywags. If they don't like the government, maybe they should go to Earth and see how well they like it there."

I blinked. He didn't deign to explain himself, but I gathered he was complaining about the daily news and another caper of the Juniper Society, the scallywags au courant. I had to agree with the Colonel—the restless spirit of the disenfranchised youth seemed excessive and ridiculous given the freedoms and choices made available by society. A rebellion wasn't necessary and wouldn't affect change unless they stopped their gin-induced scheming in the dead of night and opted for more traditional venues. It pained me to see so much promise wasted.

And it pained me to think of Earth.

John joined the table finally to my utter relief. As usual, he held a mechanism to something or other in his hand and a tool in the other. He set them down and filled his plate as he wished us good morning and inquired of his father's health.

It was shaping up to be a rather ordinary day until Gideon entered the room. I'd never seen him at breakfast before. His father and brother also looked surprised. Gideon stopped behind my chair, and the space behind my head thrummed uncomfortably. He reached over my shoulder and pilfered my cup.

I didn't turn. I didn't dare. The scent of his shaving cream seemed like a caress, and his presence was far too close, which he knew.

Gideon set the cup in front of me after drinking a third of its contents. "I knew you weren't hopeless. Not one of those weak tea drinkers. I like a girl who can drink the kind of coffee that puts hair on your chest."

I pursed my lips and didn't respond—only stared at the coffee still sloshing in my cup.

"Stop teasing the governess, Gideon," his father admonished, not bothering to look up from his PEAD.

Gideon liked to take little intimacies with me whenever he could, the kind that I could scarcely make a fuss about without drawing more attention to his bad behavior and embarrassing only myself. He lived to fluster me—picking invisible lint from my dress, pushing a lock of hair behind my ear, whispering inappropriate remarks in my ear. I chose to ignore him, but my heart pumped extra hard in his presence just the same.

"I hear there is another missing maid from the Havendish Estate," Gideon said.

The Colonel grunted.

"I see. Is another missing woman of no consequence?" Gideon asked. "Is it because she is merely a maid or that she is female that draws so little interest from you, Father."

The two of them began their circle of arguments that never went anywhere but to further prove their mutual disappointment.

Another missing maid. There seemed to be an unfortunate pattern of missing women lately.

I stared at the eggs on my plate, no longer interested in eating the congealing lump. An unbidden memory of what gnawing hunger felt like gripped me, and I quickly resumed eating, pushing away the cobwebs of my childhood. Violet Merriweather was nothing if not pragmatic, after all. Skipping breakfast would hardly help find the missing, and neither would remembering what it felt like to starve.

I had no intention of reliving those days. Life, for me, didn't begin until I'd been transported to New Geneva. I'd never been hungry at the academy. But, then, I'd never been full, either.

My station at Thornfield was downright luxurious. Good, healthy, and abundant food, a wardrobe of sturdy, well-fitting clothes, and a purpose and young charge I adored. The Colonel ignored me for the most part, but had given me freedom of the manor and a position in life I could be proud of.

I was blessed, really.

Amid the chatter between the men on the news of the day, I ate the eggs, but they didn't begin to sate the memory of my hunger.

Chapter Three

THE SUN GLINTED off the thin crust of snow, covering the path ahead of me like a trail of a thousand diamonds. I loved winter. I inhaled the crisp, clean air—its freshness something I would never take for granted. There had been no such thing on Earth. I pushed aside the momentary lapse into my old life. It wasn't worth considering. This is what I had now, and it was glorious.

"Violet!"

I turned towards the voice and smiled as John met me on the path. He cut a dashing figure, even bundled in his heavy woolen coat. , the fog of his breath seeming to crystallize before it disappeared. As always his smile was contagious. It seemed to me he should always be smiling.

"You forgot your scarf," he explained as he pulled it from his jacket and wrapped it around my neck.

And though the intimacy should have felt awkward, it did not. "Thank you."

"Do you mind company this morning? I know you like your early morning walks, but I've a matter I'd like to discuss with you."

He offered his arm, and I settled my hand into the crook of his offered arm. "I would love the company, though I must warn you, the temperature seems to be dropping. I think we're in for another snow."

He nodded and we continued on the path, our boots crunching companionably along. "Will you be staying with us for the holiday, or do you have family to visit?"

Family. I shook my head, blinking away thoughts of a baby boy I barely remembered; only that I was somehow responsible for him and I had failed. "I have no family."

John reached up and squeezed my hand gently. "I apologize. I forget that the academy is an orphanage. It was quite rude of me to bring it up."

"It's of no consequence, John. I'm proud of my upbringing." I smiled at him reassuringly.

"As well you should be, Violet, for you're a shining example for the rest of us. And I'm selfishly glad we'll have you for our own this season."

His words meant to make me feel included, but did the opposite. I didn't belong with the Winstons. I was in their employ. Perhaps I could arrange a visit to the academy, but the thought made me feel lonelier still.

"You had something you wished to discuss?" I asked, hoping to lead him away from the current topic.

"Yes! Yes, I do. Tell me, Violet, has Phillip exhibited a strong tendency towards math and science, I wonder?"

John's interest in his brother's education warmed my heart. "Young Phillip is more than proficient in both. I daresay he'll pass my own efforts inside a year."

John nodded thoughtfully. "I was the same at his age. It was hard for the governess to keep me interested, though. I wondered if you would mind if I helped."

"Helped?" I stopped in front of a bench.

John brushed the snow from the seat for me and we rested while he explained himself. "I have some ideas. If I were to engage him in a bit of tinkering with me, perhaps building toys from drawings, he would be able to go beyond the book learning. I found that taking apart and putting together makes the science more fascinating."

Considering that John was almost always distracted by one of his tinkering projects, I knew this to be true of him already. "It's a fine idea, John. And Phillip would enjoy the time spent with you as well. I only ask that you don't allow him in your laboratory unsupervised. I've heard stories about your experiments from the staff and I wouldn't want Phillip to access incendiaries just yet."

John blushed beneath the pink of his already cold cheeks. "There may have been a few small explosions in my youth, but I'm much more careful now. And it's been months since I've set anything on fire." He tugged on the end of my scarf playfully. "I like that you're so protective of my brother."

"Of course I am."

"Not every governess is as caring as you. Believe me, Gideon and I went through several."

"I can only imagine. Was Gideon as difficult a child as he is a man?" I stopped myself. "I'm sorry. I shouldn't have said that. It's not my place to criticize your brother." I was more than sorry; I was mortified. I'd had years of training and yet my boot found its way into my mouth just the same.

"Don't apologize. Gideon is...difficult."

"I shouldn't have said anything."

"My brother has had a harder life than you know." John paused to scan the horizon for the right words. "I wish things could have been different for him."

I scoffed and then regretted it immediately. "I'm sorry, John, really I am. It's not my place. It's just that your brother has been given the same opportunities as you, yet squanders his life. I can't feel sorry for him. You must know he has it better than so many."

"You judge him harshly, but you can't understand...he would kill me if I told you—"

"You mustn't feel you need to, John. I don't deserve your confidence."

John looked at me carefully. It was obvious that he loved both his brothers very much. John was a good man. A solid one. He was a little distracted at times, but he had such a good heart.

"But you do, Violet." There was a beat of time that slowed between us, holding the moment in detail so that I could relive it later. I looked away first, so John continued speaking. "You see, my mother and my father...they had a bit of turmoil after I was born. I don't remember it, I was too young, but you hear things. It was a difficult relationship; I don't think they were in love." He scanned the horizon again. "They were apart for a time, with separate residences in the city. They reconciled shortly after my mother showed signs of childbearing. I didn't understand, for many years, why my father treated Gideon so differently. I used to try to fix it—include my brother when Father spent time with me—but there was, still is, a huge wall. He always referred to Gideon as 'your son' when he spoke to my mother. Do you understand what I'm trying to tell you?"

I swallowed. Gideon wasn't the Colonel's son. "It's not my business, John. Every family has secrets."

"His whole life, Violet. The Colonel has treated him like an interloper his entire life. He was a young boy, an innocent. I'm glad my father stood by my mother despite her condition, but where was the compassion for her son? Gideon grew up thinking he wasn't worthy of attention or love or even respect. My mother tried her best, but a boy needs his father. He claimed Gideon as his own in public, but never in private. When our mother died in childbirth with Phillip, Gideon was lost."

The cold seeped into my bones, but I didn't want to leave. The story broke my heart. But Gideon was a man now, and responsible for his own fate. I rested my hand over John's. "You feel much responsibility for both your brothers, but you were a young boy, too. Gideon will have to find his way on his own. We all have things to overcome. He needs to find the strength to do so. If our childhood dictates our entire life, then I may as well give up now."

John met my gaze. "You're very strong, Violet. Like our mother. You would have liked her, and I know she would have loved you." He squeezed my hand. "I should get you out of the cold. I'm sorry for putting my family secrets at your feet this way. I suppose I simply needed someone to talk to." John stood and helped me from my seat. "Gideon blames me for being the 'good' one. I've tried to bridge the gap, but I'm not sure I ever will."

"You're a good man, John. But you can't change Gideon any more than you could change your father when you were a boy. The best you can do is what you're already doing."

The wind picked up then. Snow began falling in a swirl around us. As John escorted me back to the house, I wondered if things would ever be right between the brothers.

The scowl on Gideon's face when he saw us together at the door made me doubt it.

Three days later, the storm had not let up. We were snowbound, but there are worse things than being trapped in a sturdy, if imposing, manor such as Thornfield.

John brought laughter to our lessons. Phillip would often sit on his lap as they tightened screws and turned gewgaws, both wearing magnifying eyepieces strapped to their heads. While they worked, I would read—sometimes advanced math volumes to better teach Phillip, but often novels of dubious value. I quite enjoyed those, probably more than I should.

On such a day, the wind howled outside the windows but the liquideous aether flames in the fireplace warmed the chill. I sank deeply into the cushions, holding my new brass eNovelizer closely so that no one could see the daring book I'd chosen that afternoon.

The eNovelizer was benefit enough of my job—had the Colonel elected not to feed me I'd still be happy to work there for the electromagnetic reader alone. It felt like it was made for my hands. The readers at the academy were cumbersome, sharp, and had to be shared—this one had a buttery soft leather cover and the copper casing was smooth and rounded.

And it had my name etched into it. I'd never owned anything outright before. I traced my finger over the lettering and sighed happily.

"Such domesticity," Gideon declared from the doorway, interrupting our afternoon.

I stirred from my lounging position on the davenport, but he quickly moved in, picking up my feet and placing them in his lap in a most indecorous fashion. I struggled to pull my feet from his iron grasp from beneath the afghan covering my legs, but he held firm.

"Let go," I murmured, trying not to draw attention.

Instead he slid one hand around my ankle.

As much as I wanted to protest, the stroking of his thumb on the inside of my ankle, though too intimate and wrong, felt heavenly. Little impulses zipped up my legs.

"You're being indecent," I said lowly from the corner of my mouth so as not to attract the other Winstons.

"Am I? I thought I was being friendly."

"Too friendly."

He laughed and released my feet, which I promptly curled under me. Unladylike, mayhap, but much safer nonetheless.

"I don't mean to take liberties, Violet. It's just that you seem like such a part of our family now that I forget my manners. Wouldn't you agree, John?"

John and Phillip raised their heads simultaneously, both looking ridiculous with their huge eyes behind their lenses. "Gideon, I didn't hear you come in. What am I to agree to?"

"I was just telling Violet how brotherly we both feel towards her."

John blushed. "Yes, of course." And he bent back over the whatzit he and Phillip were working on.

I didn't like being a pawn in Gideon's chess game with his older brother.

He watched John and Phillip wistfully. I wish I could hold tighter to my declaration that he was in charge of his own fate, but at that moment, the sad, young boy that still lived inside Gideon was evident on his face.

He caught me looking at him and scowled at the compassion he must have read in my eyes. "Don't," he intoned lowly.

"Don't what?" I whispered in return.

"Don't look for ways to make me worthwhile, sprite. You won't find them, and then you'll blame me for wasting your time." He leered, but it was missing its usual punch.

All the same, I needed distance. I pulled my legs to the floor and walked away, making excuses about resting before tea, clutching my eNovelizer tightly to my chest to buffer the mad beat of my heart.

I couldn't fix what was wrong with Gideon, but like John, I felt myself wishing to.

It was later that night that I woke up nearly screaming, my heart pounding, and a cold sweat covering every inch of my skin. The wind howled outside my window, but something else woke me.

There again. A thump. A muffled voice. Another thump. I stared at the ceiling above my bed. There were no rooms above mine. I grasped the covers to my chest as if they offered protection. Protection from what? Phantom noise?

There was, perhaps, an attic space above me. It was on odd time to be moving things about, but it was possible. I listened intently, but heard nothing save the wind still moaning outside my window as if it were desperate to come in.

There would be no falling back to sleep easily, I knew, so I pushed off the bedclothes, shivering immediately, and pulled on my wrap. "My kingdom for a cup of tea," I said aloud.

My slippers were warmed from the aether fireplace. Instant comfort, blissful really. I felt richer than sin the moment they enveloped my feet.

Though I had no reason to hide, I tiptoed down the hall. The shadows made me nervous, and every creak and groan of the floorboards sounded like warnings. I had to get a hold of myself. The noises that woke me could have been the wind carrying tree limbs and whatnot over the roof. Still, I padded softly and listened intently.

The kitchen was a friendly place, despite the mood of the rest of Thornfield. I pulled what I needed from the larder, and what I needed included some of Cook's fabulous biscuits. I set my armful on a sideboard and turned to get a tea kettle.

A hand covered my mouth and braced me against a strong wall of man. "Don't scream."

My midnight intruder was almost gentle, but a primal scream ripped through me, muffled by his hand. And then I bit him.

"Christ, Violet." Gideon let go, and I turned immediately to him as he shook his hand. "You bit me." He examined his hand in the dim nightlight of glowing aether. "I think you broke the skin."

A blanket of red stole over my vision and I felt strangely out of my own body, unable to control its reactions. I began hitting Gideon in the chest, backing him into the stovetop. "You scared me. Why on earth did you sneak up on me like that? I thought you were an intruder."

"I'm sorry, Vi. I just didn't want you to scream and wake the house." He allowed me to hit him several more times before he asked, "Are you...are you crying?"

I wiped my eyes. "Of course not."

"Oh, hell. You are. I'm really sorry I frightened you." He pulled a handkerchief from his pocket. When I wouldn't accept it, he put it into my hand and forced my fingers closed around it.

I stared at the offending cloth and tried to force the percussion of my heart to slow. I hated being so out of control, being harkened back to the small animal I'd been when first brought to the academy. I wiped the tears on my sleeve, perversely refusing to use his handkerchief. "What are you doing here, Gideon?"

"I'm here for the same reason you are, sprite. Tea. Though, next time you find yourself unable to sleep, you could just knock on my door. I have other cures for insomnia you might be interested in." He moved around me and began making the tea, taking preparations away from me and giving me too much time to think about how scared I'd been and then how angry.

I began to shake, but tried to hide it from Gideon. My instincts told me never to show weakness in front of him. Still, I felt his heavy stare pressing on me.

"Stop looking at me," I whispered. "Please."

I couldn't find the will to pull myself together. I hadn't felt that kind of primitive fear since arriving in New Geneva. Certainly, I'd been scared at times, but not the kind of fear that locks away all other thought but that of survival. The terror that runs blood cold. I'd forgotten what it felt like to be a victim.

"Jesus, Vi." He pulled me into an embrace. I didn't fight it. I'm ashamed to admit that I needed to be touched. Maybe more than anyone in history, at that moment, I needed to be held. I shook in his arms, hating myself and hating him for understanding what I would never put words to.

I didn't want him to be nice to me. That made him complicated, and I couldn't afford for my feelings about Gideon to be complicated.

The kettle whistled, and I pulled out of his hold, stepping back and putting distance between us. He went to work with the tea, and I gathered my wits. I thought about skipping the tea altogether and retiring back to my room. It was the prudent thing to do. But, oh, how I longed for a steaming cup of comfort.

Gideon gestured me to the small table in front of the window, so I took a seat and stared at the darkness. There were no moons tonight, only a barren void past what the outside lanterns illuminated.

He set the tray between us and folded himself into his chair. I was used to dining with him at the massive table—this small nook made him seem impossibly large. He overtook everything.

As he poured with uncanny grace, he watched me closely, likely looking for evidence that I would crack into emotional turmoil again. While he seemed to enjoy provoking me most of the time, I could tell that he really did feel bad about frightening me.

An awkward silence stretched between us. What did we have to say to each other, really? I wasn't up for his goading, and I'm sure he didn't want to know about my disapproval of his wasteful lifestyle.

"Will you be spending the holidays with family?" he asked finally.

I closed my eyes, suddenly hating the small talk I'd trained so diligently for. "No. I have no family."

When I reopened my eyes, his gazed was fixed on me. His dark eyes searching for something, but what?

"So, you're stuck here just like I am then?" His voice was rich with his usual sardonic tone, but his eyes didn't match his words. "I guess we'll both have to make the best of it."

A few days ago, I might have told him he should be grateful to have a family to spend the holiday with. Now that I understood the dynamics better, the platitude would have been more than shallow, and I kept it to myself.

I sipped my tea, waiting for my bones to warm, waiting to feel like myself again.

"Do you like being a governess?" he asked.

"Very much."

"If you had your wish to be anything at all in the world, would you still be a governess?"

I sensed a trap, so I toed very carefully ahead. "Whoever is granted such a wish?"

"You're evading the question. I suppose that's what you've been taught, though, yes? Our society doesn't allow for wishing or dreaming. Luckily, if I were granted such a wish, I would find that I am already doing exactly what I would dream of."

"That must make you the happiest man alive, Gideon," I said dryly. We both knew it wasn't so.

Gideon wasn't happy, despite having no responsibilities or expectations. He may pretend to enjoy his life of debauchery and drunkenness, but here he was, drinking tea in the kitchen with the governess in the middle of a stormy night.

"You judge me very harshly, Miss Merriweather, and yet you have no idea what I even do away from the walls of this fine, respectable home." He sat back in his chair. "It's not very charitable of you."

"I have every idea, Gideon. You gamble, drink, womanize, and mock everyone who isn't doing the same."

He chuckled. "So, you do know. Still, until you've walked a mile in my shoes, do you think it's fair to judge me? Perhaps my road leads to the happiness you can't find here."

"But I am happy here."

"There is a whole world out there that you know nothing of, Violet. As an educator, don't you think you should have some experience with it? This society is stifling."

I stood, no longer interested in the tea. "There is a whole world out there that you know nothing of, Gideon. And if you think this is stifling, you should try breathing on..."

"Earth?" he finished for me.

"I don't wish to speak of it. Just know that whatever you have in your head about the ills of this society are nothing compared to what some must bear."

"I thought you had no memories of Earth."

"I don't need to remember to understand how awful it must be."

I turned to leave, but Gideon grabbed my hand, pulling me back into the vortex of his dark, shadowed gaze. "We're all children of Earth, Violet. Why is it that you must live your life as a servant? New Geneva is as much yours as it is mine." He rubbed the pad of his thumb over my skin, and I shivered. "Come with me some night. See my depravity first hand. I think you'd like it more than you think. There's a fire in your heart, Violet."

"No, thank you. I think I'd prefer to just imagine your depravity." It was the wrong thing to say, I knew immediately by the look in his eyes.

"Do you often imagine me doing depraved things, sprite?" I looked away rather than answer. He let it go. "Come with me."

I shook my head.

"You're not afraid, are you?"

Goodness but his presence was so large. He ate up all the air around me. But I wasn't afraid of him. "No. I just have no desire to accompany you."

"Oh you have the desire, all right. Maybe you're afraid you will like it too much. That once you are free for one night, you will not be satisfied to come back and be a governess to pay some debt you feel you owe for being allowed to live."

Oh, my proud chin didn't like that. Not at all. I thrust it high. "Are you daring me, Gideon?"

"Perhaps I am. I'll sweeten the pot. You come out with me and let me be your host to the underbelly of New Geneva, and I will stay home one night and play the part of the gentleman you think I should be."

I thought of Phillip, and of John, and how very much they would enjoy an evening with Gideon. This was blackmail, but how could I deprive his brothers of the opportunity? "You must be on your best behavior. You promise you'll try to enjoy your evening at home? You'll be pleasant and attentive to your family?"

"Do you promise to open your mind? That you won't look down on everyone and that you'll try to enjoy an evening with the people I associate with?"

What was I getting myself into? "Fine. But you must make sure I am not found out by the Colonel. I need this job, Gideon."

"Deal."

He kissed my hand, instead of shaking it, and my heart fluttered with a wickedness I'd not known I possessed.

Chapter Four

IT WAS FOUR nights later that the wall in my bedroom opened up.

The movement caught the corner of my eye first. What I was seeing couldn't possibly be real, but Gideon stepped through the gap holding a body wrapped in cloth.

"Knock, knock," he said.

I gaped but could form no words. A sick chill overtook me and I thought of the missing servants from the news. What had he done?

"I'm here to collect on your promise." He took a step towards me, and I backed up, searching for anything I could use as a weapon against this intimate villain. "Relax, Violet, I brought your costume."

"My costume?"

As always, Gideon managed to unnerve me completely.

He set his armload on the back of the chair and began unfurling this costume he'd spoken of. "Well, I can hardly bring you out dressed as you are, though you look fetching in your nightclothes." He held up a satiny concoction of peacock purple. "Hurry, put this on."

"You came through my wall." My senses, addled as they were, began returning. I looked down, astonished to realize I was standing in my nightgown in my bedroom with a man. Not just any man, but Gideon. "Yes, there are several passageways in the walls of this house. I don't use them often, but you requested that I not put your job in danger, and so I shan't. No one will know you've left your room." He thrust the garment into my hands. "Now, get dressed."

"I can't wear this. It's—"

"Not gray. Or sturdy. Yes, I know. But you can't wear a serviceable gown where I'm taking you. You'll wear this."

"I couldn't possibly—"

"Violet," he warned.

I sighed, taking my armful behind the changing screen. Removing my nightgown in the same room as Gideon felt illicit, even though he couldn't see me. Probably because I knew he was imagining he could see me. My entire body flushed hot as I quickly put on my underthings and leaned against the automated corset lacer. I stepped into the gown but couldn't pull it up all the way. It was then I realized it was up—just cut very low across the bosom.

"I cannot wear this, Gideon. It's indecent."

"You promised you would try to fit in. I can't take you there in one of your servant gowns." He poked his head around the screen. "It looks fine to me."

I gasped and sputtered, but he only stepped further in and began lacing the back of it for me. "Hush," he admonished, breathing the word onto my skin like paint. "I'm very good at dressing women."

"I should think you're better at undressing them...er...I mean to say that you would rather be known for....oh never mind." I was hopeless.

He chuckled lowly, and my toes curled. Gideon spun me around to look at me. "You're lovely."

I looked down at my chest. "I'm exposed."

"As I said, lovely."

I crossed my arms.

Gideon removed his coat and gestured for me to turn so he could put it on me. "What do you know about the first settlers to New Geneva, sprite?"

I shrugged into the ridiculously large overcoat. "Are we to have a history lesson, Gideon?"

"Perhaps we are." He turned me around and buttoned the coat as if I were a child. "You of course know of Michael Addison."

I frowned, wondering where all this was leading. "He invented liquideous aether and later colonized New Geneva because no one on Earth would legitimize his substitute for fossil fuels despite the depletion the planet was facing." Not until it was too late anyway. Much, much too late.

He tapped my nose. "Spoken like a true textbook. However, it wasn't just his invention. Addison was considered a lunatic, he and his friends outcasts. They were part of an alternative community that dabbled in costume play and pretended they were from the Victorian Era on the weekends. It was called steampunk, and most people thought they were slightly ridiculous."

"Why are we discussing this now?"

"Those are the roots of our society, love. Addison made a lot of money from the aether, even though it wasn't used as much as it should have been. He bankrolled a crazy plan to settle on a new planet, New Geneva, and modeled it after a theme park from their world called Disney. Only his was a steampunk theme park. It was as ambitious as it was insane. They were renegades from their own society, Violet. They had raucous parties that lasted for days and pretended to be airship pirates." Gideon took me to the wall where he pressed a panel to show me how to open and close the secret door. "As time went on, they just kept their twenty-four-hour-a-day costume party going and built a society that was actually pretty ingenious. We had a woman chancellor, you know—they like to leave that out of the history books. There were few rules and virtually no social classes, as everyone was pretty much a reject from their home planet. But as Earth got sicker, more and more people became refugees. New Geneva couldn't handle the influx of population if she didn't want to suffer the same consequences as her mother planet."

"The Reckoning," I volunteered with a shiver.

He nodded, casting his eyes to his shoes.

Nobody liked talking about The Reckoning. They were dark days in the history of New Geneva. Days in which hard decisions had to be made about who was worthy of citizenship and who would be forced back to a dying planet. There was violence and the first need for a military regiment.

New Geneva was a small planet just outside of Earth's galaxy. Too small to support all the souls that needed refuge, it was easily defended once the military disabled Earth's satellites—the crushing blow. Earth's population turned on itself and the citizens of New Geneva could only watch in horror at the carnage.

"Why are we having this discussion about history?" I asked.

"The society that you defend, Vi, is one that crept up on New Geneva out of fear. We were built on a different spirit—a rebellious one. One of acceptance of others instead of unnecessary classification. Everyone was treated equally in the first days. A gay man didn't live in fear of being shipped to a barren land. Women ruled alongside men. Children weren't raised in orphanages to become servants."

I bristled. "I would be dead, Gideon." He didn't reply, so I repeated. "If they hadn't rescued me, I would be dead. Hungry people do very bad things when there is no food available. Please understand, I would be worse than dead." I closed my eyes, but could still hear the sound of my crying brother as he was ripped out of my arms. "There isn't any food there. They eat...whatever can be caught." I shook my head. "New Geneva may not be the perfect Utopia you so desire, but my life is more than I dreamed possible."

When I opened my eyes, Gideon was whiter than a ghost. "I'm so very sorry. I had no idea."

"It's of no consequence."

He grabbed my shoulders firmly. "It is. You are of consequence, Violet. If I show you nothing else tonight, let it be that."

And then he led me into his secret world.

The dark alley smelled of standing water and grease. Shadows cast their own shadows as the night drew its fingers over the cobblestone and brick. I shivered against the recollection of a similar alleyway. The memory blinked across my mind like kinetoscope images in grainy black and white. I remembered scurrying away from the lights with the vermin whenever I heard the footsteps of men on the pavement. The sound of boots had struck terror into my young heart.

I pushed away the images. Those days were gone. No longer a helpless street urchin, I was an accomplished young woman now, a governess making my mark on a new world. I would prove myself beneficial to society.

I clasped Gideon's borrowed coat tighter to my neck and watched as he handed a grimy young boy a few bills, and the lad made off with the whyrlygig round the bend, surely never to be seen again.

"Valet service?" I asked, arching my eyebrows.

"Edmund will make sure nothing happens to it," he answered. When I made my opinion plain, he said, "He'll not make off with it, I assure you. Edmund is the stalwart type." I shook my head, but he ignored my disapproval. "Come on, then. Unless you've changed your mind."

"Another dare, Gideon?"

The slight lift at the corner of his mouth was answer enough.

Gideon knocked a rhythmic pattern on the first door we came to, and a gruff man with hands like ham hocks sized us up before he let us in. Once inside the door, we still weren't anywhere but a long brick hallway. Gideon bid me to follow him through a labyrinth of brickwork and down more rickety stairs than I dared count. At last he opened a large, heavy door and I stepped into a new world.

"Where have you brought me to?" I could scarce keep the wonder from my voice.

"It's called a ribaldery. It's more fun than a gentleman's club or those prissy parlors run by the upper crust."

A ribaldery. I'd heard of them. Ladies don't attend ribalderies. Not unless they are ladies of quite a different nature.

I looked at him in horror. "Ribalderies are illegal, Gideon. They get raided and...and...they are frequented by defilers and bounders."

"Which do you think I am? A bounder or a defiler?" When I made no attempt to answer, he leaned to my ear, his voice low and his breath hot. "Perhaps both?" He chuckled. "Welcome to my world, Violet."

Music I didn't recognize, with strong beats and amplified sound provided a backdrop for a kaleidoscope of color. So much color. Dresses, feathers, waistcoats—everything so vibrant I wondered if bits of a rainbow had broken off and landed in this lounge.

A haze of smoke clung to the air, adding mystery and a faint odor of cloves. Laughter punctuated the din, some of it sharp and mirthless, some of it bawdy, all of it loud.

The shocking gown I wore was the chastest outfit in the room. Women, many of them my age, in barely covered corsets and stockings lounged in men's laps, laughing and drinking. Some wore men's breeches, some wore stockings in colors and patterns I didn't know were possible. Their hair was done in strange shapes—braids and rolls so unlike the simple coil I wore. Some of the women wore their hair down, loose and flowing or stick straight, and more color on their eyelids, cheeks, and lips.

The men's styles resembled Gideon's, mostly formal suits that had been left rakishly disheveled. A few wore the clothes of pirates, or at least like the pictures of pirates I'd seen on lithographs. Their eyes barely rested on me, and who could blame them? The other females were so much more interesting than I would ever dare.

An exotic girl stopped in front of Gideon. The epicanthic fold of her eyelids spoke of a highly prized Asian ancestry. Pearls threaded through the shiny black hair she'd swept over one shoulder. Of all things, she wore a tightly fitted man's blue tailcoat. Her exposed petticoat and corset were more ornate than many a lady's best gown.

"Minerva," Gideon said as he kissed her hand. I looked at the floor quickly, not sure why. I didn't want to see his reaction to her, I suppose. At the academy, I was the brazen one, a leader and an original. In this place, next to this girl, I was milquetoast. "How lovely to see you again," he murmured against her gloveless hand.

"Yes," she said, less than impressed. "It's been all of twelve hours. Don't be droll, who's the chit?"

I wasn't sure if I was feeling more insulted or unworthy of her attention, so I settled for thrusting my hand out like a man and telling her my name.

It seemed better than a curtsy, at least.

Minerva started and then looked to Gideon as if she were wondering if I were serious. After a shrug, she shook my hand, both of us slightly awkward with the masculine greeting. "Nice to meet you, Violet. I'm Minerva. We don't use last names here." She returned her gaze to Gideon. "Good luck with that one."

And then she was off.

"Are you warm enough?" Gideon asked.

I knew he was teasing. When wasn't he teasing? The pink of my cheeks broadcast my temperature, and yes, it was plenty warm. However, his coat provided me more than warmth, and I wasn't ready to shed my cocoon just yet. Nor was I ready to ascertain why wearing his coat made me feel safer.

I rationalized that by wearing something of his, perhaps the rakes and cads in the room would understand that I was not alone, thus not fair game for their shenanigans. But really, if I were going to be honest with myself, it smelled nice, like Gideon. And it felt as if he cared for me by providing it.

Which made me gasp at my own foolishness, so I shucked it off immediately, baring my shoulders and low décolletage. Handing him the jacket, I straightened my spine.

"There's my girl." Gideon draped the jacket over a chair. "What do you want to do first?"

"Do?" I asked.

He put his arm around me and we wove through the crowd. The colors and sounds were so foreign. A man stopped in front of us with a glass vase of sorts. It held a murky purple mixture in the bottom and a layer of smoke in the cylinder. "Toke?" he offered.

Gideon waved him away with one hand.

We squeezed through more people than should have been in such a small space until we came to the center. On the stage, three women mesmerized the crowd with a choreographed dance number. They wore short ruffled pantaloons and their breasts near overflowed their laces. Their dance titillated the audience, drawing cheers and hollers. I was witnessing my first burlesque and it made my heart pound extravagantly.

And then I realized all three of the dancers were men.

"Where have you brought me, Gideon?" My eyes must have been as big as saucers.

He laughed and the sound of it jolted me back into reality. Gideon never laughed. Not really. He chuckled and he teased, but his humor was always tinged with a dark shadow.

The entertainment on stage was finishing up, so I reluctantly watched their finale, entranced by how seamless their performance was. The young man on the end was far prettier than I ever hoped to be, and I felt a little like I'd been squandering my femininity.

"You're frowning," Gideon said.

"I feel out of place," was the simple answer. He didn't need to hear that I didn't feel pretty.

Gideon led me further into the abyss. A man stopped me, separating my hand from Gideon's shirt sleeve. Gideon didn't notice and kept going, no longer in my reach.

"Drink on the house for the lovely lady," the man said.

I blushed and stammered a thank you, but as I brought the glass to my lips, Gideon plucked it from my hand and sent a look of warning to the man that sent him scurrying like a schoolboy. Gideon tipped the glass upside down, pouring the contents onto the floor.

"Do us both a favor, sprite, and don't drink anything unless I give it to you," he said, as if I were trying his patience.

"Why not?"

He looked side to side, as if to make sure nobody was listening, and then he bent to my ear. "Some of the gentlemen here aren't as trustworthy as I am," he said in mock seriousness.

I rolled my eyes at him. Trustworthy, hah. "I still don't understand."

Gideon frowned. He didn't like to get serious, but apparently, I was forcing him to dire straits. He put both hands on my shoulders. I tried not to shrug him off, despite feeling very vulnerable and, well, bare.

Gideon looked very deeply into my eyes. "I won't let anything happen to you. You understand that, right?"

I nodded.

"Violet, you're a very pretty girl and the people I associate with are reprobates. I know this because that's why I like them. They won't touch you if they know you're with me, but I'm still not inclined to trust them. There are tinctures floating around this place that would render you unable to make good decisions."

"Spirits? I'm not likely to become inebriated from one drink."

He shook me, just a little. "Not regular spirits. The tinctures are more powerful than that. Please, just promise me."

"Fine, Gideon. I promise I won't drink anything unless you give it to me." My voice conveyed my incredulity. "When did you become such a teetotaler?"

His turn for eye rolling. "As you well know, I don't abstain from much, Violet. And if you would like to get intoxicated, I will be happy to help you with that." His smile turned carnal, and I shivered, just like he wanted me to do. "But I'd rather not have you poisoned, so let me know if you're ever…thirsty."

My pulse stumbled over the inferred offer of quenching my thirst. It seemed that even if he weren't doing it on purpose, I found double entendre in everything he said.

"Are you?"

"Am I what?" I answered, wondering if I'd missed a question during my ruminations.

"Thirsty?" He asked innocently, with an indecent spark in his eyes.

I shook my head vehemently.

Gideon chuckled. "Come dance with me, Vi."

He pulled me into another room, a ballroom of sorts, where several couples had begun what looked to be a promenade.

"But the music—" The music was pulsating and thrumming with too much percussion.

"It's not what you're used to, but you can dance to it. I promise." Then he paused. "You can dance, can't you?"

Like a marionette to his strings, I answered his taunt just the way he wanted me to, letting my pride ruffle and overtake my good sense. "Of course I can dance. Dancing was part of the curriculum at the academy. In fact, I'm a very accomplished dancer. Probably better than you."

"I'll endeavor to stay off your toes."

I shot him a glare. I'd seen the way he moved. Graceful like a cat—or at least a cat burglar. My toes were in no danger, but I doubt he'd promise me safe from anything else.

We took our place for the Grand March. And I felt the distance between us keenly. The other dancers moved differently than I'd ever seen, making each step uniquely their own, despite the dance being the same as performed in all the parlors of New Geneva. As they strut, their hips and shoulders rolled in an imitation of intimacy. As if there were no inhibitions.

"What kind of music is this?" I asked when we met in the middle to promenade down the alley of dancers.

Gideon glanced at the musicians. "It's from the 20th Century. They called it Rock. It's a favorite here."

I faltered in my steps. "20th Century...from Earth?" How extraordinary and old fashioned. "Why are they plugged in?" The aether tubes were not connected to all the instruments, just the mandolins.

"It amplifies the sound."

Before the next dance began, we all took places in two lines, the men facing the women directly across from our partners. I kept my spine rigid to hold my dress up, but I would have preferred to shrink into the corner and hide. All the dancing I'd done had been in gray, drab gowns—everyone in the ribaldery shone like polished gems. And Gideon, the rake, was never more dashing.

I feared no tincture was necessary to inebriate my already addled senses.

He bowed deeply. I curtsied, not as deeply, in order to keep my feminine figure all the way inside my dress. He blinked at me lazily, his eyelids hooded as if he were slowly wakening from a slumber.

Even with the unfamiliar music, I was able to keep up with the steps I knew by rote. I began to feel a bit foolish clinging to the proper form when all around me shimmied and dipped, undulating their hips and making the dancing unique. Each time we met in the middle, Gideon would smirk or arch a brow or stare at my bosom. I let him fluster me for the first half of the song, but by mid-tune I actually giggled.

A part of me cracked with the giggle, allowing the scents and sounds and visions around me to absorb into the fissure. My heart pounded with a new rhythm and the dance ceased to be the polite exchange of manners I'd learned at the academy and instead became a game of dare. As we wove the intricate patterns of the dance into the floor, I focused much less on my feet—or even my body—and became more interested in my partner. His gaze felt like a stroke so that even when Gideon stopped a breath away from touching me after a turn around the other couple, my skin felt the rush of him everywhere.

No longer content to let him push and pull my feelings without retribution, I practiced a coy look at him over my shoulder as the dance dictated another pattern of movement away from each other. His eyes darkened at my attempt of flirtation, and I suddenly felt more powerful than a goddess.

The music, strange as it was, stirred me deeply. As the last pattern ended, I curtsied as low as I dared.

I'd never seen such a hungry man.

The air was charged with our mutual taunting. I should have known better than to play a game with Gideon, for we were unfairly matched. But it didn't stop me. I wet my lips and he smiled—not a witty or encouraging smile. One that meant to disarm me.

A waltz was next and before I had a chance to deny or encourage, Gideon pulled me too tightly to him and moved us around the floor as if we were one. I scarce had time to breathe. I should have pushed him further away, it wasn't proper for him to mold my body to his. Instead, I was trapped in his gaze like a hunted animal seconds before the shot.

"Relax," he intoned. His voice, gravelly and low, came from someplace deeper inside him than usual. "For one night, Vi, just forget who you are and who I am. Forget the academy and the Colonel. Nobody knows you here, and if they did, they wouldn't care. Tonight, you're the sprite that haunts my dreams. Let yourself have this one night. Let us both...can you?" His fingers dug into my hip. "You've come this far, you may as well let it all go."

His words filled my head until there was no room for anything else. And so, to make room, I had to let some things go. Things I'd held on to so tightly.

Prim was the first to leave from my head, as I let the rigidness of my body relax, allowing more freedom—my first taste of it. Gideon had an amazing command of our flight. We whirled and dashed and it was more exhilarating than anything I'd known. I greeted the rush of air and sound with giddy abandon.

Proper was the second thing I released, as I pushed further into him where our bodies touched, delighting in the fierce intake of Gideon's breath and the ignition of a dangerous light in his eyes. I became the sprite he taunted me with.

Sense was the last to leave, emptying the space so that Gideon had full command of my every thought.

A new ache took residence over my body, but what I coveted, I wasn't sure. I only know that when the night ended, I wasn't ready to let go. The ride home on his whyrlygig gave me time to process my own behavior in relative peace. I wouldn't have recognized myself in that ribaldery. Perhaps it was a harmless flight of fancy, but I feared what would become of me after such a taste of decadence. Just as one spoonful of trifle at Thornfield ruined me forever for going back to the pasty gruel served at the academy, I wondered if I would ever be able to don my gray dress and not remember what it felt like to fly while wearing a silk one.

As Gideon led me back through the maze of secret corridors at the estate, I grew nervous about what would happen next.

While he had never taken any actual liberties with me, would he expect to now? We danced perilously close to the edge of my ruin already. It would take barely a misstep to seal my fate.

I couldn't allow this flirtation to go any further.

We stopped at my secret door and Gideon showed me how to operate it from the other side. We stepped in and I turned, my mouth open to begin a litany of all the reasons why he needed to go.

Instead, I said, "I'm thirsty now, Gideon."

His eyes registered barely a moment of confusion before recognition dawned and he kissed me.

I'd never been kissed, so I have no comparison, but as his mouth glided over mine, I imagined that girls would stand in line to receive his kisses. I'd been a fool to think I flew on the dance floor. This was flying.

His lips danced on mine, coaxing a rhythm that matched the pounding of my pulse. If anyone were to find me in such a compromising position, I would lose everything—but I could not break his hold over me.

Gideon groaned and pulled away, taking a large step backwards. "I'm sorry."

"You're sorry?" I asked. My lips bruised and trembling.

"Well, no."

We stared at each other across the foot of space between us. Though it was only a step, the separation felt like a huge ravine. We both shook from wanting to cross but not wanting to fall.

"I should let you get your rest," he said and turned.

"Wait," I said. His eyes ignited, waiting for me to ask him to stay. "Your coat."

He blinked. "Right."

I unbuttoned it while he waited. He watched me like I was unwrapping a gift for him. He licked his lips and a sensation of desire I'd never experienced before hit me like waves buffeting a sea wall. I turned my back to him as he slid the coat from my shoulders, his hot breath on my nape, and felt him step back when my arms slid free.

"Good night, Violet."

I didn't watch him leave. I couldn't.

Chapter Five

THE NEXT FEW days were busy as the whole household prepared for the holiday, so I was able to easily stay out of Gideon's path. Though, perhaps, he'd been staying out of mine.

I lifted my chin out of habit. Well, that was just fine if he was. Just fine.

Phillip was reading, a torturous exercise I put him through day after day, and I was helping one of the maids, Marisol, hang a garland of evergreen boughs when Oliver entered the salon.

"Miss Merriweather, you've a guest," he said as gloomily as ever.

How odd. I turned to look over my shoulder, but couldn't let go of the garland. In the doorway, stood Mrs. Witherspoon, her hands clasped tightly in front of her. As usual, it was impossible to read any emotion in her face.

I am sure I looked a fright. We'd been decorating with the evergreen all morning—I'd be finding needles on my person for the next several days. The pins had been knocked loose from my hair leaving it half up and half down, and sap had collected on my hands and face over the hours. "Er, hello, Mrs. Witherspoon. What a pleasant surprise."

Her eyes darted from my face to the precarious step-ladder I was atop. "I'm sorry I couldn't give you more warning, Miss Merriweather. I meant to leave this note, but they assured me you were allowed visitors."

"That I am. Give me one moment to extricate myself from the indoor forest, please. Phillip, you may be excused."

His face lit up, and he wasted no time in his escape. Oliver relieved me my end of the garland and I wiped as much stickiness from my hands as I could as I joined Mrs. Witherspoon at the door.

"Shall I ring for tea, then?" I asked, wondering what I owed this visit to. I never expected her to check on my arrangements. I was of the mind that once she let one of her flock go, we were on our own, never to return to the nest.

"This isn't a social call, I'm afraid. Is there a place where we might speak privately?"

Now that really was odd. "Of course."

We sequestered ourselves in the small sitting room across the vestibule. Her eyes darted about nervously, never landing in one place too long.

"Are you doing well, Violet?" she asked me. "Do you like your post?"

"Very much. Phillip is a wonderful student and my accommodations are more than comfortable, as you can see."

Her lips pressed together in a firm line briefly before the mask returned. "And they are treating you well."

"Very well, Mrs. Witherspoon."

She didn't rush to fill the silence. The tick tocker on the wall kept track of every missed opportunity to break the awkward quiet.

She exhaled loudly. "You've perhaps heard the distressing news about the missing maid from the Havendish Estate?" Mrs. Witherspoon had never looked the picture of robust health, but her pale skin drew tighter over her high cheekbones than usual, and the bruise-purple crescents under her eyes were more vivid.

"Yes, of course."

She closed her eyes, "The newspapers mistakenly reported her as a maid. I'm so sorry, Violet. Shelby...Shelby had recently taken a position as companion to the aging Mrs. Wilkes at Havendish. That afternoon, they had been shopping and Shelby went missing. They've not found her, or evidence that she is...well."

Dots began to dance in my eyes like fireflies. I tried to blink them away but they persisted until everything around me darkened but the flickering pattern of lights.

"They've pronounced her dead. Shelby is gone, Violet."

Gone.

I tried to stand, but the world lost substance. I remember trying to say there had been a mistake. That she couldn't be gone, not Shelby. Not my sweet, darling Shelby. And then I remember falling endlessly into a graceless slumber.

When I woke up, I was lying on the sofa and John was kneeling in front of me holding a cool cloth to my forehead. I was disoriented and nauseous, so I blinked instead of speaking.

"There she is," he said, his friendly tone soothing.

I groaned, bringing my hand to the lump on my temple. "What happened?" I tried to sit up, but John pushed me back gently.

"It's better to rest a few minutes more. The doctor is on his way."

"Doctor?" I frowned. "What is going on?"

"You had a spill. Mrs. Witherspoon says you bumped your head on the table on your way down. It's a nasty lump you've got there, and you were unconscious for several minutes."

Mrs. Witherspoon. It all came back in a rush of sadness.

"Oh, Shelby," I cried. It was real, then.

John looked behind him and gestured. Mrs. Witherspoon entered my line of sight. Oh, how I wished it had been a bad dream.

"I'm truly sorry, Violet. I didn't want to leave until I knew you were all right, but the other girls..." she trailed off.

"Of course. They need you now."

After she left, I tried to go to my room, but John refused. "You shouldn't be alone right now, Violet."

I stared at the ornate plaster ceiling. "I am alone, John."

"How can you say that?" He took my hand in his large, warm one. "You have us."

I pulled my hand out of his. "I'm your employee. No, not even that. I am an employee of the estate. If I were to disappear tomorrow, the most that would be said about me is 'a maid from Thornfield disappeared today'." I finished sitting up. Slowly so he wouldn't notice how weak it made me. "I should not have forgotten my place."

"You know we don't feel that way about you. You've been here a short time, but you're important to us. Phillip is doing so well with your guidance. He's a happy boy. And I've found...I've found a friendship with you I hadn't expected. I know you are hurting right now, but you don't have to hurt alone." His beautiful blue eyes shone with concern and something else I needed to ignore.

I wished very much I could take what he offered, solace, comfort...maybe more. Perhaps, even an hour ago, had he said to me that I belonged to Thornfield and that Thornfield belonged to me I would have accepted that I belonged somewhere. Finally.

But it was too much to bear now.

Who knows what horrors Shelby faced before she died—perhaps she was still living them. She'd never done anything to anyone and now she was gone as if she never mattered at all. But she did matter. She mattered very much to me.

I blinked back the onslaught of hot tears and begged John to allow me peace. I couldn't bear to hold them back much longer, and it wouldn't do to lose control in front of my employer. He squeezed my hand and reluctantly allowed me to retreat.

The physician saw to me in my quarters, prescribing rest and a tincture that tasted like bark. The lump on my head ached some, but was nothing compared to the hole in my heart. Even though we hadn't spoken in a while, I'd taken comfort in Shelby's presence in my life. Because I had her, regardless of proximity, I was not alone.

Now I was.

I didn't sleep, take a tray, or light a candle, much less a fire. I barely moved for hours sitting in a chair and staring at the wall. Life was precarious and its sands sifted quickly through the hourglass, I knew that. I'd always known that. But for the first time in my life, I wanted to rage at the unfairness of it all.

Tomorrow, I would close what was left of the wound in my heart and carry on. Wiser, I hoped. Never again would I allow anyone to matter so much, for it was not my lot in life to depend on love, friendship, or family.

Tomorrow I would pick up the pieces. Tonight, I would grieve.

Hours later, the cold seeping into my bones became painful, but I couldn't work up the gumption to move, much less build a fire. When I heard the wall slide open, I should have been surprised, but wasn't.

"Violet, it's freezing in here." Gideon's candle, the only light in the room, backlit his face in a ghostly fashion. "What the devil do you mean to do, freeze to death?"

Perhaps Shelby was still out there, in the cold, freezing to death.

I looked away and said nothing.

He went about lighting the aether logs, muttering about foolishness and melodrama. I continued my silence strike. Once he was satisfied that the flames were strong enough, he crossed the room and dragged the quilt from my bed. Stalking over to my chair, he made quick work of cocooning me in the bed covers, and amid my protest, he scooped me up.

"Put me down, Gideon. I'm in no mood for your shenanigans tonight."

"My shenanigans?" He unceremoniously plopped me on the floor in front of the fire. "I'm not the one courting pneumonia in the freezing cold." While he spoke, he lowered himself to the carpet behind me and pulled me between his legs so that my back was to his chest and his arms surrounded me with his heat. "If you had come across one of the girls from your academy playing such melodramatic games, you'd be livid."

"I don't want to talk about the academy or anything else."

I tried to pull away, but the cage of his arms was solid.

"Then don't talk. Listen. And stop struggling. Your only recourse right now is screaming, and I doubt you want to bring the household to this current folly."

Again, the unfairness of my life filled my chest with bitterness. He was right. Gideon could do anything he liked to me. My choices were to let him or lose everything to the scandal of being found alone with a man in my room. At that moment, I hated him.

I stopped struggling.

"Good girl. Now listen to me. Your friend would not want you to martyr yourself this way. You are doing her memory no favors."

"Please go," I whispered, my desperation louder than the words.

Gideon's arms went slack. "I wish I could leave you alone, sprite. God knows. But you worry me and I'm terrible with concern. I don't know what to do with it."

That I believed.

"I'm fine." I sniffed.

He rested his chin on my shoulder. "You're breaking my heart."

"That is the first humorous thing I've heard all day."

"That's my girl." He rubbed his hands up and down my arms, warming me whether I wanted it or not.

"Gideon, you're too close. You shouldn't even be here."

Now that I was warming up, it felt as if my skin were prickling. I almost wished he'd rub my arms again, but of course didn't voice my desire. It wasn't my place to ask for things. I was to be happy for whatever I received, after all.

We stared into the fire, sharing the silence while the blaze ate the logs in a cacophony of hissing and spitting. Behind me, Gideon shuffled a bit and procured a flask, holding it in front of me, he asked, "Drink?"

"No, thank you."

"It will warm you up."

I sighed and gave in, knowing he would badger me until I did, anyway. It took a bit for me to unwrap my arms from the cocoon he'd made me, but I grasped the flask from him and sipped carefully.

Whatever it was burned a path from my throat to my belly. An involuntary shiver wracked my body. But he was right, it did warm me up. "That's awful," I managed, glad he couldn't see my scrunched up face from his position.

"That is very expensive and well-aged brandy."

"Well, it's awful expensive and well-aged brandy."

"Do you want another sip?"

"Yes, please."

We passed it back and forth another time, and then I declined the offer for more. I'd done my duty to him, apparently, as he didn't harangue me for another drink. Instead, he did worse.

"Tell me about your friend."

I shook my head violently. "I don't wish to talk right now, Gideon, please don't make me."

We were quiet for a few more moments, listening to the wind and the crackle of the fire. He broke the silence with news of the weather.

"It's snowing again tonight."

Weather, I could manage. "Oh? Are we in for much do you suppose?"

"Likely." And then. "Bloody hell. This is ridiculous. I won't carry on this inane, polite conversation. Not with you. Tell me about your friend, Violet." His tone was acerbic, but he kneaded my shoulders gently.

"Her name was Shelby."

"Have you known her long?"

"All my life." My voice broke and he turned me into his chest. And I let him.

I'd thought I wrung out all the tears I had for Shelby, but there were buckets more. Gideon held me, rocking me gently, and soothed me with more inane platitudes that would have meant nothing if they'd come from anyone else.

And then, he held me some more. Until my tears had dried.

He placed me on the bed, removed my boots and most of my clothes, and took down my hair. I let him. It was wrong of me, I know, but I let him just the same.

"What were you doing before you hit your head?"

"Hanging evergreen garland with Marisol."

"You have more sap in your hair than a normal tree would hold. Good luck getting that out tomorrow," he said. And then, Gideon-the-Heartless tucked me into my bed covers, pressed a kiss to my nose, and sat in the chair in front of the fire until I fell asleep.

And I let him.

Chapter Six

THE NEXT EVENING, I excused myself from dinner with claims of a headache and retired to my chambers. I set the fire in the grate, changed into my most worn, therefore most comfortable nightgown, and curled into bed with my eNovelizer and a heavy heart.

I'd managed to fulfill my obligations for the day without shedding a tear. Phillip hadn't known what was wrong, but knew I was upset and behaved so angelically that I missed the precocious boy I usually dealt with. Gideon had been conspicuously absent, yet always in my thoughts, and John had remained in my peripheral vision, but never intrusive, as if to say he was there if I needed him. The brothers Winston were bound and determined to tangle me despite my efforts to protect my heart from all three of them.

Though I'd loaded so many books onto my device that I'd never be able to read them all, I was surprised to see that the list had been extended by at least ten books I'd never heard of. As I scrolled the catalog, my curiosity piqued even more as they were all books from or about the 21st Century.

Earth.

Some were books about politics. Others were philosophy and history. Gideon was the only person I could think of who would sneak these books into my possession. But where had he gotten them and why was he sharing them with me?

Trying to understand Gideon was not a practical endeavor, so instead I began reading the first book on the list, a biography of Madeleine "Maddy" Austen, the first female President of the United States of America.

It was hard to imagine. Women were protected from the rigors of politics on New Geneva. Most women didn't need to work at all, unless they were in my class. The wives and daughters of our planet served a different purpose, though no less noble. They made the world a better place by gentling the harshness of the lives of their working men. They added beauty and serenity with their hearts and sensibilities. When the men came home, worn out from their work, it was to the women they returned to for comfort and respite.

Women were more delicate than men.

Even as I thought it, I heard Gideon's voice in my ear. If that were so, then why was I not as fragile? What of Mrs. Witherspoon? Or the countless women who did work because they were not born to a station above it? Was I less delicate or, perhaps, were the women considered so actually more robust than appearances determined?

Maddy Austen hadn't been born to privilege. She'd been a single mother trying to make a living in a poor economy. She and the other mothers in her neighborhood would trade childcare with each other, and often met for coffee in her apartment home. It was there they christened her dining room the "round table" and what began as jokey lists for changing world problems somehow became a manual for a better world.

Maddy appointed many of those mothers to her cabinet when she made it all the way to the pinnacle of American politics. She'd been passionate about many things and was widely recognized on Earth as one of history's best leaders.

She'd championed green technologies as well. It was unfortunate that she couldn't rally as many supporters of her environmental initiatives as she did her social ones.

I glanced at the aether logs burning in the grate and tried to push back the memories of the consequences of Earth's fatal denial.

I don't know why living at Thornfield had brought back my memories with such force. I'd hardly thought of Earth the entire time I'd lived at the academy. It wasn't until the day of the sale that the tumbler in my brain brought the remembrances up over and again. It seemed the harder I tried to push them away, the stronger they became.

I closed my eyes and heard the boots of men, heavy on the pavement. Even scared as I was, I'd had to keep my breaths shallow or risk coughing. I used a rag to filter the air, but held it over the baby's nose and mouth instead of my own. There was shouting. A scream in the distance and another much closer. When the baby cried aloud, I knew we were done running.

My heart raced and I got out of bed, pushing the memories away. Not tonight, not on top of everything else I was feeling. I needed a distraction, and quickly. I dressed in haste and used the secret panel.

Gideon's whyrlygig was quite easy to maneuver even without any lessons. I managed to follow the same path to town he'd used, much faster than the pneumatic taxi's route, and, better yet, it avoided the sentry at the wrought iron gate. I even found his street urchin on the curb, ready to help me.

"I don't have any coin, Edmund." I hadn't planned very well. I hadn't planned at all.

"'sallright," he answered. "Master Gideon pays me ahead sometimes, so he doesn't have to worry about carrying money. I'll take care of you."

We both knew Gideon didn't pay him "ahead" for his own convenience. He was obviously trying to keep the boy afloat. "Gideon speaks very highly of you, Edmund. I can see why."

The boy beamed as he made off with Gideon's transport, hopefully not for the last time. I set myself to the same foot path as before. I'm fairly certain I didn't know the right signals at the door, but I was recognized by those that mattered and they let me into the ribaldery with no fan fair.

I wore the same dress as the last time, though it was my own cloak, not Gideon's, that I held together tightly as I soaked in the rowdy atmosphere. I dismissed the pang of regret that I should miss him, the scent of his cloak. I sat on a barstool facing the room instead of the bar man, better to watch the antics.

The colors and sounds were fascinating. On stage tonight was not the female impersonator group, but one very real, very feminine woman dancing. She shimmied her jeweled hips in a skirt of sheer fabric. On top, she wore a contraption that covered her breasts, barely, with scraps of fabric and jeweled ties. The men sitting near the stage were mesmerized by the sway of her body, loose and lithe, under the colored lights. I blushed when she touched her own skin, caressing herself in a way that should have been vulgar, but seemed instead to be almost beautiful.

What must it be like, to feel so about one's body? She had no shame in her feminine figure or grace, and while the men ogled, they seemed reverent. I wondered if Gideon had watched her dance before. If he'd compared me to her. No wonder he teased me so.

I was a priggish miss. Why had he ever bothered to bring me here? Or kiss me afterwards. When he tucked me in last night, did he leave Thornfield and come here to watch a real woman? Had he ever touched her? Kissed her the way he'd kissed me?

"Miss Violet, whatever are you doing here tonight?" Minerva had sidled up to me while I was lost in thought.

"Hello, Minerva," I managed, feeling somehow as if she'd caught me. As if she'd known what I was thinking.

She'd donned a long sheath that evening. It was cut so trim I'm not certain how she walked. The material of her dress was forgettable, but she accessorized with so many strings of pearls she must have cleaned out an ocean. Her hair fell long and straight, completely unadorned, but her eyelids were painted like rainbows.

"You didn't answer my question. Where is Gideon? I didn't think he was here tonight." She slipped a long string of pearls through her fingers absently and studied me. I had a feeling it was impossible to get anything past Minerva.

"I came alone."

One of her eyebrows shot up in a perfectly sculpted arch. "I'm not sure how wise that is."

I tilted my head at the assumption. "Tell me, Minerva, do you have an escort this evening?" For she seemed very much a woman who did what she pleased.

She smiled wryly and ordered two drinks. "I don't need an escort. I live upstairs. No dangerous travel required."

As she passed me a drink, I remembered Gideon's warning. I stared at the glass while her cool eyes bored into me. "Maybe you're wiser than I thought, Violet. Gideon would kill me if I let anyone spike your drink, though."

In for a penny, I thought to myself, and sipped the amber liquid. I scrunched my face as it went down. Brandy again. "I doubt he would kill you."

"I prefer not to take the chance."

We watched the dancer and sipped our drinks in companionable silence until the song ended. "Why are you here?" she asked baldly.

"Why is anyone here?" I countered.

"Are you looking for Gideon?"

A sidelong glance told me she was staring as if to unearth my darkest secrets.

"If you've designs on Gideon, Minerva, I can assure you, you'll brook no arguments from me. We have no attachment."

"Really." She seemed amused. "It seems to me you must have a tie of some sort. He's never brought anyone to a ribaldery before."

I shook my head, willing her to understand. "He just seeks to fluster me. He thought it would be a great lark to take a fish out of water."

"You have a lot to learn about men. I'm not certain that Gideon is the best beginner model, but I wish you luck."

As I opened my mouth to protest, we were interrupted by a deep, male voice. "Imagine my surprise to find my whyrlygig had gone to town without me this evening."

I spun to face my accuser. He took the glass from my hand and sniffed it before handing it back. He exchanged telling glances with Minerva, and she smiled as if she'd not only eaten the canary, but possibly one of its friends as well.

Then he trained his gaze back to me and the heat left my face. "Gideon—"

"Dare I ask what you're doing here?"

"She's having a drink with me," Minerva answered. "Want one?" she asked, the playful tone of her query caused an answering, visible throb of his temple.

"I'm sorry I borrowed your transport without asking, Gideon. I didn't think you would need it as I thought you were already out and had taken a coach."

Minerva leaned back on her stool and sent me a saucy wink. She was not helping matters at all. If it turned out that Gideon really were furious, I risked losing my job.

Of course, I'd already risked my employ by sneaking out at night. I may as well enjoy it. I began unbuttoning my cloak.

"Not that little number again. Gideon, you have the fashion sense of a ...well, of a man." She grabbed my wrist. "Come with me, Miss Prim."

Despite my protest, and Gideon's, she dragged me to the stairs, up a flight, and into a small room. Material of every color hung from any available piece of furniture or knob. A huge vanity alit with bulbs of aether was covered in pots of color and brushes of varied size.

She rummaged through a rack of clothes until she found what she was looking for and then sent me behind the privacy screen.

I looked at the garment she'd thrust in my hand and began a very emotional protest. "I simply cannot wear this."

"You must. That color of red will be amazing with your skin tone."

"It's a corset. It should go under a dress, not become my dress."

"Violet, do you want to stand out? Because if I were you, and I were visiting a place where I hoped no one recognizes me, I would want to blend in. If you want to blend in, you must not look like a lady sneaking into ribaldery. Own thyself, love."

She had a point. And the color was perfection. I'd never seen anything that shimmered quite as much.

After I came out, she gave me an approving huff and sat me in the chair at her vanity. Before I could manage a word, she'd undone my hair. It held the waves from drying in coils, so she pulled it to one side and adorned the other with a comb decorated with peacock feathers.

"Close your eyes," she demanded.

"Why?"

"So I don't blind you." She began dusting my eyelids.

"Why are you doing this?"

"I have poured blood, sweat, and tears into building the reputation of this ribaldery up. I won't have people thinking we no longer enforce a fabulous code."

"A fabulous code?"

More dusting, this time on my cheeks. "Yes, only fabulous people with wicked sensibilities are allowed. You have the spirit, but not the wardrobe."

"I have the spirit?"

"Gideon wouldn't bring a useless moppet with him. He's as much to lose from his reputation here as you do in your world if you were found out." She did something to my lips with a special quill. "Now, are you going to tell me why you came without him tonight? And why he looks at you with such concern?"

I was still absorbing the idea that she thought I had a fabulous, wicked spirit, so it took me a moment to formulate an answer. "I needed a distraction. To not think."

"Why?" She surveyed my face and picked up another pot of color.

"A friend...a friend of mine is missing. They believe her to be murdered."

She raised a brow. "The maid from Havendish? You're not a lady then." She took in the new information with the kind of concentration John used for numbers. "Interesting."

"She wasn't a maid. She was a companion. And her name was Shelby." It was important that they get it right. "Why did you think I was a lady?"

Minerva shrugged. "You're so cool and collected, even when he's trying to ruffle you. I figured maybe you were married to some old lout and Gid was tempting you to the dark side or something."

"I wouldn't have been the first married lover he's seduced, would I?"

"Well, he doesn't tumble with unmarried girls, if that's what you're asking. He's not a despoiler of the virtuous, as a rule." She paused, realizing I wasn't married. "He hasn't..."

"No!" I answered, perhaps a little too emphatically. "We haven't...that is to say...we aren't...he doesn't like me that way."

"Right."

"Like you said, I'm an unmarried girl. Not his preference at all."

"I'm certain that isn't true," she said as she spun my chair around to face the mirror.

My breath hitched. "You're a magician."

While I was not used to color on my face, it didn't look harsh. The kohl around my eyes sought to define them, but not obstruct them. My hair looked as if she'd spent hours on it, not seconds. And the corset...

I'd never thought much of my chest. It was there, it did its job with the pushing and pulling of air into my lungs. My breasts would never nourish a child, so I really never thought much about them, other than the fact that they ran on the smaller side.

The corset pushed my breasts up, of course, making them suddenly much more ample than they used to be. The color of the fabric did indeed look nice with my coloring. I thought of the woman dancing on stage and a strange, alien sensation stole over me.

I wanted Gideon to see me like this.

"You're not going to fight me on this, are you, Violet?"

I didn't even want to blink, lest I shutter myself from my reflection. "No, Min." I swallowed. "Thank you."

I'd surprised her. She watched me watching myself for a moment. "You need gloves."

She went in search of a specific pair that had somehow gone into hiding in a drawer. Once found, she unrolled the black lace onto my hands, pulling them all the way to just inside my elbow. "You're going to out-fabulous everyone else out there." She paused. "I'm sorry about your friend, Violet. Shelby was lucky to have you to remember her." There was more to say, but she shrugged away the serious tone. "Gideon will probably faint when he sees you. I hope you carry smelling salts because I sure as hell don't have any around here."

Chapter Seven

GIDEON WAS STANDING at the bar when I descended the stairs. He brought his drink toward his lips, but stopped midway and stared. I hoped he was staring because I looked pretty and not because I was an oddity one might find at the Cirque de Freaque that came around once a year.

I'd never felt pretty before. It was certainly not something I strived for. Pretty was for other girls, girls less concerned with survival. I had always desired to be practical. Practical and well fed.

The man Gideon had been speaking to wondered where his attention had gone and followed Gideon's gaze, his eyes widening with appreciation as Gideon's narrowed with…something else. I resisted the urge to tug the corset up. Minerva warned me that she'd slap my hand if she saw me do it.

It was suddenly very hard to breathe.

A different man, dressed in six or seven shades of green approached as I got to the bottom. He bowed, making a great show of it, and picked up my lace-covered hand, kissing the back of it. "If I may be so bold as to ask for a dance?"

"Not unless you want to die in the most painful, merciless way I can come up with. And believe me, at this moment, my imagination is fairly robust." Gideon took my other hand, leading me away. "Come, sprite, I've given the band all my liquor money for the week if they promise to play only waltzes for the rest of the evening."

The other gentleman grimaced but put up no argument. I had a feeling no one liked to tangle with Gideon, though I didn't find him all that imposing myself. He led me through the crowd, his hand firmly squeezing mine as if I might bolt.

Once we reached the dance floor, he locked me in a tight embrace and we took flight, the colors and sounds whirring past me as Gideon deftly twirled me through the other dancers. I wasn't as self-conscious this time, as my outfit made me fit in much better, just as Minerva had said it would.

Gideon hadn't said anything to me yet, so I tried to break the ice and loosen the mask of irritation he wore. "I want to apologize again, for the whyrlygig. I don't know what came over me to think I should just take it. I wasn't feeling quite myself, I suppose."

His face softened and he pulled me closer. "If you must know, I was never really angry. Mostly just intrigued. You continue to surprise me. I expected that I'd have to devise a fiendish scheme to get you back here, and you trot off and come on your own."

"I shouldn't have."

"It wasn't safe. I'd prefer that you allow me to escort you on your nightly rambles." He shushed me as I tried to argue. "I'm not trying to inhibit you. I can stay out of the way, if you like. I just don't want you to be hurt. Until they find whomever...I'm sorry. I don't want to ruin your outing with that kind of talk."

A coldness leeched into my bones. "You're right. It was foolish of me to go alone. Until they catch the killer, I'll only go out if you accompany me."

It didn't escape either of us that I hadn't suggested that I not go out.

"Thank you for the books, though I'm not sure why you chose the ones you did."

"Really?" he asked, spinning me in an impromptu break of the waltz pattern. It was so like him to spin me out of control during something I knew by heart, and yet, it was fun to give up what I expected and see where he would take me.

"Well, if you must know, I prefer scandalous novels to history."

"I'll keep that in mind. Most women would prefer flowers and fripperies, but I knew better. I'd get nowhere appealing to your vanity, so I aimed for your intelligence. Books for my Violet. Give the reading a try, though, sprite. I think you'll like it. They're from my personal collection."

They were books he'd read. That he'd shared them with me felt more personal than if he'd given me a lacey undergarment. I'd go over them more carefully now, searching for clues about what made Gideon's clock tick. How many people even suspected that he read, much less what he read about?

"It's like I can see the cogs and wheels of your brain spinning. What has you so rapt all of the sudden, Vi?"

"I'm wondering if those books are an answer to a riddle."

"What kind of riddle?"

"One that explains you, sir."

Another spin. "I'm not really that complicated."

"Oh, but you are."

"I think you are the more interesting of the two of us. For instance, you pretend that you believe what society tells me about you, and yet nothing could be further from the truth."

"What exactly does society tell you about me, Gideon?"

He waltzed me out a side door into a dank, musty corridor. We stopped moving when he pushed my back to the wall and left not an inch between our bodies. "Society tells me that you are meek and malleable. That your sex needs to be quiet and biddable and that your station in life must keep you invisible. That I am somehow a better person than you because I can open jars and was born rich."

He pressed against me harder and my senses heightened unbearably. His body so firm against my wielding softness. Every place we touched set off sparks, kindling a dangerous fire. His gaze traveled to my displayed cleavage and back to my lips, where it lingered, before meeting my own again.

"But we both know none of that is true. You're worth one hundred of me on my best day." He ground the words out in a voice so deep, I felt the baritone of it in my fluttering stomach. "You pretend to go along with a society that tells me you're somehow less because you were born female, but deep down, you know it's not true. Why is it that you think it's better to go along with them when they seek to control and subdue you?"

I couldn't think of anything but the way he could control and subdue me using his voice and the press of his body. He stared at my lips again, groaned when I couldn't stop myself from licking them. I arched my back to get more contact. "What are you doing to me, Gideon? I can't think. I don't even want to."

His hands moved up my sides, cupping my bosom, squeezing gently. "You're the sweetest temptation. Every day I have to talk myself out of taking you, making you mine. I try to rationalize that if I just get it done, I'll be able to move on, get over this constant longing. Is that what you want? Do you want me to take you? Here? Now? Against this wall?"

Yes. Yes, of course that's what I wanted. Everything in me screamed for him to find his pleasure in me. But I'd crossed too many lines already. I had very little of worth in this world, I needed to protect my virtue.

He noticed when the sanity returned to my eyes. I read the disappointment in his, but something else, something that caused him to say, "Good girl," when he banked the fire of lust in his eyes.

He was proud of me.

The next day, I struggled to stay awake during Phillip's history lesson. Gideon had the luxury of sleeping the day away after a night of rabble rousing, but this governess did not. John took pity on me after a rather unladylike yawn and whisked Phillip to the lab for an impromptu science lesson.

I tried to read some more but found myself dozing a bit when Oliver handed me a note from John. I'd been invited to the laboratory.

Most often, I tried to stay away from John's lab. When he was in it, he became distracted and consumed with whatever he was working on, so it was usually a useless gesture to visit him there. I often worried that he'd forget Phillip was even with him, but I was assured by my charge that John was always most attentive on their shared lab days.

I knocked and entered the huge space with tables of boiling liquids and automated who-knows-whats. Beakers and glass tubes lined the tables and I coughed a little at the smell of sulfur. At least, I hoped it was sulfur.

Phillip was wearing a white coat that matched his brother, and they had both donned safety glasses. I was glad to see that John had taken me seriously about eye safety. Also, the matching coats were adorable. John was so good with him. It was a shame that the Colonel devoted so little time to parenting, but Phillip was exceedingly lucky to have John.

Phillip smiled when he saw me and ran over to grab my hand. "You'll see! You'll see!" he yelled and led me to a small glass Petri dish. "I know you've been sad, so I wanted to make you something. John helped. But not too much because I'm a big boy."

"Of course you are," I replied.

He and John very seriously mixed some things from droppers and vials into the dish. One more dash of something, a slight pop, a puff of smoke, and an excited little boy squeal of delight later, above the Petri dish hovered a hologram of a perfect violet.

"However did you do that?" I asked.

"Perhaps someday I'll tutor you, Miss Merriweather," answered John, looking as pleased with himself as Phillip did.

"It's a violet. Get it? Violet is your name," Phillip added.

"It's beautiful." And it was. "Thank you so much. If you can tell me what letter violet starts with, you may have the rest of the day free from studies."

After the correct answer, Phillip cleared out as fast as his little legs would allow. I offered to help clean up, but John would have none of it.

"It's your gift. You can't clean up after a gift."

I smiled. "Thank you for helping him, John. It means so much to me that you've taken such an interest in his education."

"He was adamant about making you something to make you feel better. He told me your weakness was chocolate, but I doubted you would eat anything from my laboratory."

I laughed at the truth of it. "I don't know how he came up with such a thing. Chocolate?"

"I imagine he noticed that face you make when you eat the cakes at tea. I've certainly noticed that your favorite part of dinner is dessert."

"What face?" I asked incredulously, laughing in spite of myself. It felt nice.

"It's quite noticeable," John smiled, but a faint blush tinged his cheeks. "It's almost as if you were anticipating a kiss."

Now it was my turn to blush. "I'm certain you are exaggerating."

"Perhaps. But likely not." He busied himself with a vial. "Are you doing all right then, Violet? I've been worried about you. Your friend, the maid—"

"Companion."

"Sorry. Companion. You were very close?"

I nodded.

"I'm sorry to hear that. I know what it's like to lose someone close." He placed his warm, solid hand over mine. "I don't ever want to go through that pain again."

The words were unsaid, but they didn't need to be aloud. I wasn't sure how I felt about him insinuating that he cared for me. A part of me felt warmed by his sweetness, but another part cooled.

It wouldn't do, in any case, to be found in a compromising situation with John any more than with Gideon. I needed to extricate myself from both brothers.

"Thank you." I pulled my hand away.

"You're afraid to feel too much. I know how that is. I made a pact to never let anyone into my heart again the day my mother died. But with time, the healing will come, and one day you'll realize you're ready to take a chance again."

"I'm certain this conversation is not appropriate, John."

He grasped my elbows and me toward him. "One day will happen, and I'll be here Violet."

"John—"

"I'm sorry. I know my timing is horrible and you aren't ready for this now. But I'm staking my claim. When you're ready, I'll still be here."

He kissed my forehead and strode from the room.

What a mess I'd made.

One brother, sweet and warm, would have been an excellent match were I born from different circumstances. The other, dangerous and unnerving, would never do in any circumstance. But it was Gideon I thought of when I repeated John's words in my head.

My heart, it seemed, had already been staked.

Chapter Eight

THOUGH THE HOUSE was alive with candlelight and greenery, it was missing its heart and it never showed more than on Christmas Eve. All the candles in the world couldn't light the shadows of Thornfield.

Gideon chose Christmas Eve to stay home and fulfill his end of our midnight bargain. I thought it was cheating, as he should have stayed home Christmas anyway, but I was assured by careful inquiry of the household staff that it was, indeed, something new to have him there, awake and sober, on a holiday.

As I helped the maid, Jeanette, finish decorating for a small party, the Colonel stopped in the parlor.

"Miss Merriweather, why aren't you ready?" he asked gruffly, already seeming to be walking backwards out of the room as if my answer had no consequence.

"Colonel?"

"For the party." He shook the bulldog at me. "You need to get ready. You can't very well wear that."

I looked down at my dress, perfectly acceptable for the activity I was currently pursuing, and purchased by the Colonel in any case. "Colonel, I'm not sure I understand. You expect me to attend your Christmas party? I'm the governess."

"I fail to see why I need to explain myself to you, Miss Merriweather. As you say, you are merely a governess. Put on a frock and do something with your hair. My sons don't seem to know how to act in company without your presence." He huffed and spun out of the room.

I was aghast. "I most certainly did not say merely a governess."

Jeannette giggled, and I slapped a hand over my mouth. I had not meant to say that aloud.

"Do you have a party frock, Violet?" she asked in good humor.

I shot her a look that I expect she read quite well. Neither of the outfits I'd worn to the ribaldery were suitable, and according to my employer, neither of my serviceable gowns would work either. "No."

"Come along then." Much like Minerva, she grasped my wrist and led me to her quarters, stopping to inform a maid or two of the new happenstance along the way.

In her chambers, the ones she shared with two other girls, I was placed in a chair. Jeannette reached under the bed and brought out a dusty box tied with twine. "So much for Clare cleaning under the bed regularly," she said as she blew the dust off. "This will be perfect. Take down your hair while I shake the dress out."

I doubted it would be perfect, as Jeanette was three inches taller and blessed with curves one could barely see around. I started removing pins as she untied the string and pulled out a gorgeous green dress. It was nothing like the outfits Minerva had in her room, but it was lovely nonetheless.

Too lovely. The fabric must have cost a fortune considering Jeanette's wages.

"The dress is very dear, Jeannette. I can't possibly borrow it. You should save it for a special outing."

She smiled like a woman with secrets, and she patted the dress. "I've had my special outing in it. Besides, where would I wear it now?"

Her eyes went someplace else, for a bit, and then she trained them on me with full concentration. Once again, I was to be made anew by another person and another new dress. Jeanette called upon Marisol to do a quick hem once the gown was on. Jeannette herself brushed and coiled my hair into coronets, and then pinched my cheeks for color.

Was it just the other night my face had been painted for the same reason?

As she threaded sprigs of baby's breath and dried roses into my hair, she suddenly looked years younger. She was actually getting excited. As if she were getting ready for a ball rather than attending to me for a dinner party. We'd never been close and I didn't deserve her rapt attention any more than I'd deserved Minerva's.

"Why are you helping me?" I asked.

"Why wouldn't I?" Jeannette answered. "We women need to stick together. Especially now..." Her voice trailed off.

Especially now. She was right. "I can't tell you how much I appreciate it. I'm sure the gown looks much better on you. I wish you could go in my place."

She and Marisol thought that was uproariously amusing. "I'd rather do just about anything than go to that Christmas party," Jeanette said when she could catch her breath.

"Is it that bad?" They only laughed harder "Why must I go?" I asked, sounding very much like Phillip.

"If you thought the Colonel was bad, wait until you meet his sister. She's a pill that one."

I smoothed down the fabric and looked at myself in the mirror. The dress actually was perfect. After the hem and well placed clip to shirr the fabric, I looked more than presentable. And completely different from the other night. It was as if each new day, I found something new in my own reflection.

"Who else will be there?"

"Lady Leanna, probably. The Colonel's been trying to marry Master Gideon to her for going on two years."

I held my facial expression very still to not arouse suspicion. "Oh? What is she like?"

"Beautiful. Icy. Rich," answered Marisol. "The usual."

"Are they courting?" My heart plummeted down, down, down, even as my mind wagged a finger and an I told you so at it.

"Master Gideon is very cordial to her. You know what that means."

I smiled because otherwise I would cry. "That he'll marry her." Of course he would.

"Heavens, no. That man is only nice to women he has no use for." Marisol nodded to Jeanette for confirmation that I was done, and by silent agreement the three of us headed out the door.

"I don't understand." We walked down the hall and stopped at the stairs.

Marisol squeezed my shoulders. "Sure you do, Vi. He's a scallywag, though I'd defend him to my death, I would. The ladies his father parades under his nose are not the kind of women he likes."

"What kind does he like?"

"Not the kind that he'll meet in his father's parlor, that's for sure," Jeanette answered.

As we made our way down the stairs, I realized, once again, that my foolish heart deserved every crack it gained from caring how the rest of the conversation went.

"Does he trifle with the staff, Jeannette?"

"Heavens, no. He just associates with women who the Colonel would hate."

I suppose I was relieved at that. "Why doesn't the Colonel try to marry John first? Isn't he the eldest?"

"There's been plenty of that, to be sure. But Lady Leanna has shown special interest in Gideon, if you take my meaning."

I felt nauseous. Had I really thought I was special?

We stopped down the hall from the parlor doors. That was as far as they'd be going with me it seemed.

"Have a nice time, dear," Jeanette said, and they both chortled as they walked away.

I took a deep breath and rounded the last corner. John joined me the instant I stepped into the parlor, as if he'd been waiting. He bowed. "You look lovely."

I tried on a winsome smile. "Thank you, John. I feel a bit peculiar, though. I'm not sure why your father was so insistent that I come."

I felt the heat of Gideon's gaze from across the room and tried to pay attention to John's answer while my insides melted like candle wax.

"You've been good for our family. I'm sure he just wants to make sure you feel welcome."

John introduced me first to his Aunt Edna, though he failed to mention that I was in the family's employ.

She scrutinized me carefully. "You'll do," she said, echoing her elder brother's declaration of me.

From the corner of my eye, I beheld Gideon speaking with what had to be Lady Leanna. She was beautiful, and anyone in the room would proclaim their matching dark looks would beget handsome children. And all the while he appeared to be the perfect gentleman, I saw Gideon as I never once saw him with me.

Bored.

John rescued me from his Aunt Edna's continued scrutiny by suggesting that I meet Lady Leanna. I felt it was like rescuing me from a snake to pit me against a lion.

We met in the middle of the room, each of us on the arm of a Winston brother. After the formalities occurred, Lady Leanna sized me up as if perhaps she wondered how she'd get the stain of me off a good lace table cloth. She tightened her clutch on Gideon's elbow and pursed her lips. "How very fortunate I am to have another woman here this evening. So often, I'm the only unmarried female at Thornfield gatherings."

She looked anything but pleased. I rather suspected she preferred the attention.

As if remembering his manners, John said, "Let me get you a drink, Violet. The cider is quite good."

"Thank you," I replied, not missing the subtle arch of Gideon's eyebrow.

Alone with a barracuda and a shark.

Gideon spoke first, "You look lovely this evening, Violet. The green of your gown matches your eyes."

"Thank you," I replied, not missing the subtle arch of Lady Leanna's eyebrow.

Hurry back, John.

"Will your family be joining us as well? I'm not acquainted with any Merriweathers."

"No," I answered, not filling in any blanks.

"Violet lives here. She's Phillip's governess," Gideon supplied.

"Oh." She blinked her surprise.

Gideon watched me with stony countenance as I blushed. I shouldn't have come. I needed to stop playing dress-up games and pretending to be someone I'm not. I'm not sure what he wished to do with that answer, other than give her ammunition.

Lady Leanna thought for a moment and then handed me her empty cider cup. "Perhaps you can take this back to the kitchen for me. I'm done," she said, and walked away.

My lower lip trembled but didn't hold back the biting tone of my words. "Why did you do that? I didn't ask to come. I didn't want to be here. Why would you humiliate me like that? I thought…I thought at the very least we were friends."

Gideon plucked the dirty cup from my hands and placed it on the nearby mantel. "Why are you humiliated? She's the one who should be ashamed of herself. Did you see the way she treated you? Close your mouth, sprite. Gaping is very unattractive."

"You set me up!" I whisper-shouted. "You just had to put me in my place. Was it that important to you that she understand I am merely a governess?"

I tried to storm away in an indignant huff, but Gideon stepped in front of me. "I'm sorry. I meant to prove a point about this society that you refuse to condemn. I didn't mean to hurt you. Only to show how shallow they are and why I want nothing to do with them."

"You are that society, Gideon. You think you're above them, but you're not. All your ironic posturing aside, you have the power to change things but you don't. You'd rather just complain about indignities of a class you don't know the first thing about. If it's so awful, do something about it."

Oblivious to the tension between us, John brought me a warm cider. "Ho, there."

I took the drink and willed my face to cool down from what I'm sure was a fiery red. From behind his back, John produced his other hand, in it a chocolate biscuit. I blinked back a tear. He was sweet. Sweeter than I deserved.

"Thank you, John. I adore those, as you know."

Gideon stared at the chocolate in his brother's hand as if it were a large insect. He looked at me, and then at John, and furrowed his brow before he walked away.

"Where is Phillip?" I asked. "Surely he should be down by now."

"Phillip doesn't come to this gathering."

For the second time in so many minutes, my jaw dropped. "Why ever not? It's Christmas. This is his family. Though not Lady Leanna. Is she?"

"No. Her father is close friends with mine. The two of them come to many of our gatherings."

I shook my head to get back on the correct line of thought. "Regardless, Phillip should be here."

"Violet, nobody wants to be here. We certainly don't want to subject a boy to it."

The honesty of his answer shook some of my righteousness off. "How likely is it that claiming a headache will get me out of this dinner? I'd much rather eat with Phillip."

John smiled and offered my treat again. "That's a capital idea. However, if I must remain, you must remain."

The warmth of his smile reached around and pulled at my heart like a magnet to steel. "Let's sneak him dessert then."

An inner light of mischief came alive in his eyes. "Consider it done."

Dinner was a somber affair, especially for a Christmas party. Even the mock parties we held for practice at the academy were more spirited.

Lady Leanna made sure the conversation never strayed far from Lady Leanna. Gideon pushed food around his plate but kept his glass refilled several times a course. The Colonel spent the meal complaining about the Juniper Society. And John squeezed my hand under the table.

My eyes widened in surprise. Was he trying to be supportive or was he flirting? I didn't know how to handle myself in the situations John and Gideon kept putting me in.

As if my straying thoughts tapped his shoulder, Gideon raised his eyes to mine.

Maintaining what suddenly seemed liked intimate eye contact with me, Gideon leaned his head towards Lady Leanna so she could whisper something in his ear. Jealousy tasted bitter and rancid as the bile of it bubbled inside of me.

He was trying to make me jealous.

It was working.

John poured more wine in my glass and I thanked him, grateful for a reprieve from Gideon's games. As I touched the glass to my lips, Gideon raised his to me as if in toast. As if to say touché.

Did he think I was using John to compete with Lady Leanna? Perhaps a part of me was. No, no I liked John. I liked him very much, and I never led him to believe that I was interested in more than the camaraderie of friendship.

John had never stolen liberties with me. I doubt he'd even think of disrespecting me by visiting my bed chambers in the still of night. He'd never push me against a wall to kiss me, or undress me, or do just about any of the things Gideon had done. I blushed thinking about those things. How I'd wanted them. How I wanted them again.

I looked to Gideon again and found him staring at me with a hunger he should have reserved for his uneaten dinner.

Lady Leanna noticed it as well.

"Miss Merriweather, hadn't you better check on Phillip at some point?" Lady Leanna asked, reminding everyone, in case they'd forgotten, that I was staff and not guest.

"Yes, of course." I stood, glad of the excuse to leave the miserable party.

"Violet—" John stood, embarrassed for me.

"Please, stay. Enjoy your supper." To the table I said, "Christmas tidings everyone. I must go see to my charge."

The men stood. All but Gideon.

Chapter Nine

"WHAT ARE YOU doing here?"

Perhaps it would have been a question better asked while he was still outside my bedroom door, before I'd stepped aside and let him in.

While I was becoming quite used to conversing with Gideon in my bed chambers, it seemed ever so much more illicit when he came in through the door, rather than the wall. My heart kicked at my ribs violently, sending my blood on a hot, strange new course through my veins.

I leaned heavily on my door, the solidness of it grounding my spirits some, but kept my hand firmly on the knob for instant escape. He shouldn't be here. I shouldn't have let him in. I don't know why I ceased being practical whenever I was alone with Gideon. Or perhaps, I knew exactly why, which was the much more frightening prospect.

I wanted to be alone with him. Part of me craved it. Even as angry as I was with him, and I was plenty angry.

He hadn't answered yet. Instead he stared at me. Glowered, more like. His gaze was like smoke, obscuring everything but the heat that kindled in his eyes. "You know why I'm here."

I suppose I did.

My hand was damp with sweat and slipped off the brass knob I'd been holding in a terror grip.

"Why don't you go visit Lady Leanna?"

"I've had more than enough of the pleasure of her company."

"Well, she certainly seems to enjoy yours."

"Jealous, sprite?"

I shrugged. "She's the perfect match for you. You're each just as pleasant to be around as the other."

Gideon laughed. "Your claws are sharp tonight."

He took a step towards me, and I held my hand out as a halt. "You should go."

"Leanna means nothing to me. She's not the one I dream about at night."

"You should go," I repeated, though my voice shook more this time.

"Is that what you want?"

I closed my eyes, hoping to find the strength there to say yes.

Or perhaps no.

Gideon stepped closer, his scent wrapping around me. He'd been riding. The smell of horse and leather and midnight combined with the trace of bourbon and his shaving soap. Growing up in an all-girls academy didn't prepare me at all for the sensations so much masculinity brought with it. It permeated every cell, tinged every one of my thoughts until I was no longer just me without him.

I opened my eyes with no discernible change in my temerity.

He was close enough to touch me, but I don't think I'd ever felt further away from him. We stood on opposite cliffs, the valley between us promising a dangerous fall. Who would be first to jump?

"You're frightened of me. Of this," Gideon said. I didn't have to ask what he meant by this.

"Of course, I am." I ignored his look of hurt. "Oh Gideon, we both know you're going to hurt me."

He drew his brows down, unable to find the lie to make me feel better. I swallowed hard around the lump lodged in my throat.

"I should go," he said, but made no move to do so.

He drew unsteady breaths. Was he nervous too? No. Of course not. Gideon had nothing to lose.

"It isn't fair," I said, reacting to my own realization.

"What isn't fair, sprite?"

"You have no consequences. If you stay or go—you lose nothing. If you're found here, you lose nothing. Who would even slap your hand? My ability to provide for myself—my reputation, my livelihood—everything can be taken from me just by you standing there. Even if I say no to you, if someone sees you here, I'm done."

Gideon reached into the abyss between us first. Using only his finger, he brushed a lock of hair from my cheek. "I'm a cad. I don't have to tell you that. But you know I would never take unnecessary chances with your reputation."

"You are right now."

"No, Violet. I said unnecessary chances. I couldn't stand one more minute without this chance, this night. It's wholly necessary." He became enamored with the jumping pulse point on my throat. "I can't give you the things you want, Vi. Stability, a home, a husband, a family—none of that is within my power."

"I don't want a husband."

"Yes, you do."

"You barely know me, Gideon. You don't know what I want."

He chuckled, low in his throat. The sound pulled at something in my center, loosening me from my moorings. He cupped my cheek, his palm warm and sure. I felt hot and cold and full and empty all at the same time.

"I know you, all right. I know you like I'm looking into a mirror at my own soul. I see the things you hide, and I feel the things you want. And you want the husband and the house, Vi. But more than that, you want me."

I inhaled sharply, like I'd come out of dream. He stared into my eyes, waiting. Waiting for me to invite further advance or turn him away. God help me, I couldn't do either.

"I may be a bad man, Violet, but I won't take what isn't freely offered."

I couldn't say the words. I couldn't say any words. I stared at his mouth, letting time stretch taut between us. But Gideon was no gentleman. He may not take me against my will, but he had no compunction about removing my will altogether. He brushed the hair completely off my shoulder and pressed a kiss at the edge where my skin met the neckline of my bedclothes. "Tell me to go," he warned, his breath so hot on my neck. He zeroed in on my pulse point and I gasped his name. "Tell me to go," he repeated, his voice tightened with barely repressed fervor.

"I can't."

"Then tell me to stay." He pulled back and the cool air misted my skin where his mouth had just been. "I can't tell you about love, but I can teach you about passion. It's inside you. Right now it's screaming to me. I've heard it since the day I met you, Violet. Tell me to stay."

"I can't," I cried. Trapped between a longing I didn't understand and the need to protect myself, my station. I couldn't win. "I'm not strong enough."

His mouth twisted into a grin that was neither happy nor cruel. "Now you're lying. I've never met a stronger person than Miss Violet Merriweather." Gideon stepped back. "I should leave."

My future flashed before me. Gideon would not be in it. And neither would this tumultuous frenzy, this dance with danger that made my blood sing. If I wanted a taste of passion, this was my chance. I grabbed his arm as he made to walk past me. "Stay."

Without a word, Gideon swooped me into his arms and carried me to the bed. Once again, the storm in his eyes thrashed me about like a pebble in the rolling sea. There was nothing for me to hold to that wouldn't send me under the waves. I wanted to drown in the way he made me feel until there was nothing left of me to wring out.

He didn't ask if I was sure, if I understood what was to happen. He trusted that I knew my own mind, my own body, and that made him even more irresistible to me. That he assumed I had agency over my own decisions, not doubting that I knew what was best for myself, turned up the flame under my skin, so that when he laid me down on the mattress I immediately reached back up and drew him into the first kiss ever initiated by me.

Gideon didn't waste a second on surprise, but returned the press of my lips with his own ardor, ardor built up the long weeks we'd been denying this night. Our tongues met in a sweet duel from which we would both perish and then be transformed. I needed him closer, needed to feel the rush of his skin beneath my hands. I was too far gone to be shocked at my desire as I yanked his shirt from his trousers to get at the hot flesh beneath it. He sensed my urgency, pushing my greedy hands away to pull the shirt over his head.

Suddenly unsure, a moment of shyness made me pause with my hand a scant inch from his chest. I looked to Gideon for encouragement. He brought my hand to his lips and kissed it before placing in over his heart. I flattened my palm against him, the dark curls crinkling under my palm, and closed my eyes, letting the host of new sensations have their way as I was hopeless to do naught but allow them their due.

"Sprite, you undo me." He pulled me into an embrace, an embrace that felt more intimate than all the open mouthed kisses we'd shared. He surrounded me, his arms, his scent, his heartbeat.

I tasted the skin of his neck, his groan signifying a tender spot behind his ear, so I spent more time on it until he shivered and began gathering my nightgown in tight fistfuls. Fascinating. That I had so much control over him with my untried passion was very empowering, so I kissed his mouth again, taking the whisper of my name from his lips to my own. We maneuvered together in an unpracticed waltz to unfurl the gown from my limbs without breaking our kiss. And then, he pulled it over my head.

Though I was naked, Gideon's eyes didn't roam but stayed firmly locked with mine. The intensity of his stare was more effective than the peeling of my clothes. He stripped me bare of all the things I thought I needed to cling to. It wasn't my skin he exposed, but the woman inside of it.

He began with a soft kiss on my temple. Moving slowly, he pressed another towards my jaw, stopping for a quick nibble on my earlobe. I shivered mindlessly when he suckled my neck.

I didn't know there were so many places on my body directly connected to the place where my womanhood clenched, but Gideon knew. He mapped each nerve ending with his tongue and his lips and an occasional light scrape of teeth. His busy fingers traced soft whorls onto the sensitive skin of my torso as his kisses marauded south. He spent eons of time kissing me until I was a slave to need.

"Please," I begged.

"Please what, Vi?" He nipped at my earlobe, and I cried out, so he took my mouth in an intimate kiss, thrusting his tongue into my mouth. I met him push for push, sliding my hips in a primal rhythm that matched our kisses.

And then he went back to my neck.

He was going to kill me with painful, painful pleasure.

"Please what?" he repeated. His hand finally cupped me below and I shamelessly rocked against him. "Tell me what you want."

Though he was happy to take my virginity, he didn't want a passive lamb led to slaughter. But how could I tell him what I wanted when I wasn't sure myself? "I don't know."

"You know."

Bastard. "For God's sake, Gideon. Take off your pants."

He chuckled and rolled away to sit at the edge of the bed and remove his boots. He was too far away, so I crawled across the bedcovers and allowed myself the bold pleasure of kissing his back.

His skin was hot and I let my hands roam, enjoying the hot planes of his muscles and the way he shivered under my administrations. I craved to know everything about his body. Gideon was perfectly formed for my pleasure. He was seducing me by sitting still, of all things.

Overwhelmed, suddenly, by the intensity of all that I was feeling for him, I wrapped my arms around him and laid my chin against his shoulder. We were skin on skin, my chest pressed against his back. For a moment, I thought he might end the embrace, but he dropped his head back so we were cheek to cheek and held my arms tightly to him.

In that moment, I was closer to Gideon than I'd ever been to another person my entire life. Not just physically. A bond had formed whether I wanted it or not. I had thought maybe I could give him my body and nothing else, but I was wrong. So wrong.

The prim governess and the reckless playboy. Who'd have guessed they would understand the other so perfectly, if only for one night?

Even as I knew better, I allowed the moment to proceed. I breathed him in, let him settle into my soul as if he belonged there.

It was going to hurt when this affair had run its course. It was going to hurt badly.

Gideon sighed. "You feel entirely too good."

"I was just thinking the same."

"I'm going to do the most wonderful, terrible things to you very soon. I'm going to make you so hot you'll burn out the sun. In just a few moments, that is." And he tightened his grip.

"So far, I am enjoying being debauched."

We remained silently holding each other for a few minutes more. And it wasn't until my hand began caressing the firm muscles of his abdomen that he reached around and pulled me into his lap. His hands grasped my hips, grinding me into him while he kissed me like I was the last drink of water on a planet gone to desert.

I felt no shame in my nakedness, despite the fact that Gideon still wore his damned pants. I felt as if I'd been set free. I didn't have to be Miss Merriweather with Gideon. I was all the things he'd told me he seen in me from the start. I was in control of my body, my pleasure, and it felt delicious.

I broke away from the kiss, ignoring his protest. "Take off your pants or I swear I'll kick you out of this room."

He lifted one corner of his mouth in the grin that always undid me, and in one move flipped me onto my back. I rose to my elbows to watch as he stood and shucked off the last thing between us, and my bravado tempered at the sight.

"Gideon..."

"Relax, Violet."

I pulled my legs beneath me and scooted up to the pillows. "Perhaps we can go back to embracing for a bit."

He crawled over me to the other side of the bed. "I promise it will be fine."

"It won't fit. It can't possibly."

"Oh Violet, you've just increased my ego to ungodly proportions."

"It's not your ego I'm worried about."

He traced whorls over my skin with one finger again. "We were made to fit. You'll see."

I wouldn't have believed him, but he began raining hot kisses over every inch of me until I was hot enough to put out the sun, just as he'd said. I was back to begging for him to fill the ache he'd put in me from that very first day.

"What are you doing, Gideon?" I asked as he nuzzled the seam where my legs met my body. "Surely you don't mean to..."

"Oh, I mean to. I definitely mean to." He presented me with an open mouth kiss and I nearly bucked us both off the bed. "Relax, sprite."

"Relax, he says."

He chuckled.

No part of me was safe from his clever tongue. Not my breasts as they filled his mouth. Not the backs of my knees as he spelled my name by tracing each letter into my skin. And not the place where a woman hides all her secrets.

He brought me to the edge of the world more than once. Setting me free to tumble in the stars over and again. When I no longer knew if I'd ever come back down, he entered me slowly though his body was wracked with uncontrollable shivers and it was clear that his patience was costing him dearly.

He paused after breaching my maidenhead, waiting until my body became accustomed to him. "The moment I saw you, I knew you'd own me, Violet."

But I never could. We'd have this night, but that was all. Our paths should never have crossed.

He'd go on someday to marry a fine young virgin his father chose, and I'd drift away to another position in another house.

Neither of us wanted to find love, not with each other, not with anyone else. I would never trust that love could last, and Gideon would sabotage anything good that came his way.

But really, amidst all the tragedies of a dying planet and one struggling to regain its humanity, ours was just a little sorrow.

Chapter Ten

INSTEAD OF DISAPPEARING into his world of shadows after our night of intimacy, as I'd expected he would, Gideon surprised me by spending even more time at Thornfield. I didn't know what to make of his decision, but his constant presence kept me in perpetual arousal, despite that he never returned to my chambers.

He'd always been too intimate with me, but his teasing had new meaning now. When he stood too close, I ached for his arms. When he stared at my lips, I longed for another kiss. When he slipped a double entendre into dinner conversation, a visceral memory of his naked body against mine would paint a blush over my cheeks.

And, so, in the interest of making him as miserable, I began devising Gideon's torment.

One morning, as he joined us for breakfast, I toed my slipper off and ran my foot up and down his leg. He sputtered into his coffee and raised a brow. I returned with an arch of my own and stared at his lips. A far away gazed overtook him, as if he were reliving a pleasant memory. To taunt him further, my tongue peeked out for a quick slide over my lips, wetting them.

A small groan escaped him.

"Are you alright, Gid?" John asked.

"A bit of a headache is all," he replied as his breakfast plate suddenly became so interesting he dare not raise his eyes from it.

"That's what you deserved for drinking as much as you do," the Colonel said, not looking up from his PEAD.

Gideon's face fell. He'd been home for several nights in a row now, dining with the family, playing cards with John and Oliver before retiring at an appropriate time. His father barely noticed his presence and yet damned him for his past behavior even when he was not out carousing.

My heart ached for him, for his emotional angst played over his face before he replaced it with his usual sardonic mask. He desperately wanted his father's approval, though he'd never admit such a thing and would never dare court the approval with action.

John, sensing the downturned mood, began a conversation about the weather, but Gideon excused himself anyway.

The Colonel slammed his hand on the table after a few more minutes of reading from his PEAD.

"The rabble rousers again, Colonel?" I asked, in an effort to be polite.

"Miss Merriweather, if I wished to discuss politics with the governess, I would have hired a man," he shot back at me with a somewhat surprising amount of venom.

"Yes, sir." I stared at my plate while the heat of humiliation scored me within. As it was customary for me to take solitary walks after breakfast, I was able to exit a few moments after without causing suspicion.

I found Gideon in the stables. Despite the winter chill, the stable was warm. Gideon had removed his jacket and undone the top fasteners of his shirt. Instead of announcing my presence, I watched him work for a few moments, reveling in the grace and economy of his unhurried, fluid movements as he groomed his horse.

"You're being curiously quiet, sprite," he said, though his back was to me.

I should have known there was no sneaking up on the hunter. I stepped further into the barn. "I didn't want to disturb you."

He turned to look at me then, and my pulse raced at the sight of his exposed neck, somehow tan against the white of his lawn shirt despite the vampire hours he usually kept. I wanted to kiss his skin, the spot where I knew I could make him tremble.

"You seemed very much set on disturbing me earlier. You were very close to becoming my personal buffet at the breakfast table, propriety be damned."

I strolled in, conscious of his wary stare. He joked, but he was hurting. Like so many women, I guess I wasn't immune to the siren call of a man in pain. It summoned me in its gravitational pull, entreating me to balm his wounds and nurse his heart.

"You haven't been back to my room. I thought maybe my charms were lost on you."

He huffed, not a real laugh, but closer. "It's been killing me to stay away."

I stood very close to him, close enough to touch him, and yet I did not. "I would welcome you." It was a simple statement, and yet, it felt as if the words contained every hope and fear I owned.

He set the brush on the rail and devoted his full attention to me. He then hesitated until my hands found their way to my hips, and I was about to reach for a very unladylike tirade. Putting his hand over my lips, he started, "I was very careless with you, sprite. I went to your chambers to seduce you, yet did nothing to prevent a babe from being conceived."

I jerked my head back. "You needn't worry. I'm sterile."

A small gasp escaped his lips before he recovered. "I'm sorry. Was it...because of Earth?"

"All academy girls are sterilized at age twelve." I shrugged, believing it to be common knowledge.

"What?" Gideon practically exploded. "They force barrenness on children? And this is okay with you?"

"Nobody knows what ills we could have brought from Earth inside our bodies. It is safer for the continuation of humankind that we not procreate and plant a scourge on this planet as well," I argued, though there was no anger behind my words. It made perfect sense to me.

"You sound like a brochure from the Ministry of Health." He shook his head, balling his fists. "It's unconscionable. I don't see how your academy girls don't start an uprising for the injustices my society has reaped upon you."

"I'm sorry. Would you rather I be pregnant right now? For heaven's sake, it worked out for the best, didn't it?"

"The best, Vi? Truly? What if you marry some bloke in a few years and want a family?"

"I don't intend to marry, as I've stated to you before. And if some random bloke steals off with my heart someday, I expect he'll understand that we won't conceive children and be fine with it."

"It should be your choice." He brushed a hair from my eyes. "No one should have the right to take it from you."

"What about my choice to be your lover?" I reached for his jaw and stroked the place where tension caused him to clench it so hard. "I enjoyed making love with you. I like how you make me feel." I brought up my other hand to cup his face. "I'm asking you to be my lover, Gideon."

His eyes flew open and the angst I'd seen earlier had been replaced with a fire. "You're positively the sexiest woman I've ever met, Violet Merriweather." Gideon grasped my hips, and ground himself into me. "I wish I could make you understand how you make me feel. I wish I understood it myself. You stand there in your sturdy gown and touch my face and I melt. You tell me you enjoy making love with me and I feel like a god. The fact that you stand there and tell me plainly what you want is the most erotic pillow talk I've ever heard. I want you. I want to be your lover more than I want my next breath. But I don't want to lead you on a winding road, Vi. I can't promise—"

"We'll make no promises, then. Each night is a gift."

"I may make a promise or two." He nibbled my earlobe, and the sensation shot to my center, melting me like a caramel from the inside. "I promise to make you howl with pleasure. I promise to spend hour upon hour attending to the backs of your knees where you tremble at the slightest touch."

My eyes rolled back into my head remembering how he'd turned me to jelly with his wicked tongue and the backs of my knees. "And so it begins," I said. "But for now, I must go torture your little brother for hour upon hour with my evil maniacal devices like books and letters and numbers."

"You say the filthiest things."

I turned but Gideon grasped my hand and kissed it. I walked away, accomplishing my goal of mending Gideon's heart after the episode with his father. And most assuredly setting my own up for breaking.

Three weeks later, a lucky break in the weather meant my day off could be spent in town rather than Thornfield. I had a bit of coin saved up and wished to shop. I'd never been shopping for myself and quite looked forward to it.

I hadn't known I'd be earning a wage until a purse made an appearance on my nightstand. At first, I thought Gideon had left it, and shame burned from my roots to my toes. Later, I noticed Oliver delivering a similar purse to Cook and realized it was my pay. On top of room and board and the PEAD and the eNovelizer, I was earning a wage.

I wished all I could feel was pride, but even though it had been an error, I couldn't get past the feelings that somehow Gideon had paid me for my body. I knew my morals were questionable by allowing myself to become his lover, but the idea that I would be his mistress plagued me. Why should I feel so differently if money were involved? And was I going to let it cloud what we had now?

What did we have now? Certainly, we enjoyed each other's company. He read to me, sometimes, while we were naked in my bed. More than once, I'd fallen asleep to the timbre of his voice. Always in the morning he'd be gone.

It didn't do any good to ruminate on what we had or didn't have, so I shook myself off and spent a few hours looking at bits and bobs for my hair, lacey things I might tempt my lover with, and perfumeries in which I might find a signature scent. No matter how hard I looked, I could find nothing that interested me in the least. I wondered where the ladies I'd seen at the ribaldery had found their costumes, because it certainly wasn't where I was looking.

As I crossed the cobblestone path, a small mewing stopped me cold. My heart raced as I recognized it as human and a sound that I remembered well from my youth. Crying, the hopeless, desperate kind that came when all was lost and death was waiting.

I wanted to run, which shamed me, so instead I followed the sounds to the source. A woman, maybe a girl, lay on her side, hugging her knees to her chest in the alley. Her face was covered by a mop of unbound hair tangled around itself like a thicket. Her thin dress was no match for the winter chill, and full of dirt and holes besides. She wore no shoes, which had been the most heartbreaking part until she lifted her face and I saw her dead, sightless eyes.

I crouched down in front of her shivering form. "There now," I said in a soft voice. "My name is Violet. What's yours?"

She didn't answer but shrank into herself even further on a moan. She'd been battered, her bruises calling out the ugly violence she'd seen. I looked around for help, but saw only passers-by who refused to return a glance. And then I noticed where we were.

"I have friends here, friends who can help you. Do you think you can walk?"

She shuddered. "Why? Why would you help me?"

"Goodness, why wouldn't I help you. Can you stand? If you stand, you can put your weight on me and I'll walk for the both of us."

"Go back to your manor and leave me alone."

"That simply won't do." I recognized pride when I saw it, for the poor woman raised her chin as I'm wont to do. "I suppose I could drag you across the way, but I'm afraid it might hurt you more. If you could just stand."

"Lady, I'm a whore. Ain't no one going to help me."

I narrowed my gaze on her, knowing that I wasn't far from her status. One misstep and we'd be sharing the same fortune. "I won't leave you in the street."

Though it pained her terribly, we managed to stand her up and hobble to the secret door of the ribaldery. I knew I would catch the dickens for this. The ribaldery was a secret and to visit in broad daylight would put everyone at risk, but I had little choice.

I thought Minerva would spit nails at me, even as she asked the bouncer to carry my new burden to a room upstairs.

"What the hell, Violet?" she asked.

"I'm sorry. I didn't know what to do. I'll tend to her wounds myself."

I started towards the stairs when Minerva stopped in front of me. "You've risked my livelihood and your own for someone you don't even know. I may as well put a sign out advertising."

"I don't think anyone saw me," I explained, though lamely I'll admit. "I couldn't leave her to die in the street, Min."

Minerva sized me up with that calculating stare.

"She can't tell anyone where I brought her, she's blind."

Minerva glanced away from me to hide the feelings she didn't think I knew her to have. "She would have left you."

"You don't know that."

She rolled her eyes. "She needs a doctor."

"Do you know one who will come here?" I pulled out my coin purse. "I'll pay him."

Minerva stared at my money. "You're an odd one, that's for sure."

"I prefer original."

"I'd strangle you myself, but Gideon is going to brain you a good one when he discovers what you've done."

I thought of the young woman who'd faced such violence upstairs and knew I'd never know the same fate from the hands of Gideon. But he couldn't protect me from the rest of the world, not forever. If I were smart, I'd plan an alternate course.

Minerva sent for the doctor, well, as close as we were going to get anyway. He was an addict who'd lost his licensing several years prior, but worked for cash for those who stood no prayer of being seen by a real man of medicine. His hands were shaky, but he was fastidiously clean.

I paced the floor while he saw our patient; the tea Minerva poured grew cold. I wasn't sure I trusted this doctor, but I had very little training myself. Min sighed at my anxiousness and put me to work polishing glasses behind the bar.

When the doctor came down, Minerva stood next to me while he recited the litany of contusions and broken bones to us. She reached for my hand and squeezed as the list went on and on. The blindness, near as he could tell, was hysterical in nature. Whatever she'd seen had traumatized her enough that she didn't want to see anything else again.

There was little we could do for her but clean her up and let her rest while she healed. The doctor's parting words were that she wouldn't be able to return to her "employment" for some time as she'd been raped as well as beaten.

After he'd gone, I looked up the stairs and steeled myself to face the poor girl. What was I going to do with her now? I couldn't take her to Thornfield.

"Sit," Minerva demanded as she poured us both a glass from a crystal decanter. "You look like the angel of death right now."

I sipped the alcohol while Minerva tipped hers back and shot it down in one swallow.

"I don't know what to do." I believe that was the first time I'd ever said such a thing. I used to be the go-to-gal when things went amiss.

"She can stay here for a few days," Minerva announced. "But you need to stop trying to save the world. You're going to get all of us in trouble."

I wanted to hug her, but I knew better than to thank her profusely. Instead I nodded and refilled our glasses, slamming mine back the way she'd done.

When I finished coughing we got quiet again. "Who would do that to another human?" I asked, mostly to pierce the silence.

Min shook her head. "Don't go down that road, Violet. People are capable of more than you know."

I shuttered my eyes as the moment the baby, my brother, was wrenched from my arms all those years ago chose that moment to replay. I knew exactly what ills people were capable of. But I also knew the good, and that was what we needed to concentrate on.

Minerva and I tended our new charge together, sponging her gently as she moaned.

"What's your name then?" Min asked her.

I didn't expect her to speak, but she ground out, "Lily."

"Do you have any family, Lily? Anyone who..."

"Cares? No. I told you in the street that I'm a whore. Nobody gives a damn what happens to me. Nobody even tried to stop him from taking me."

"Are you one of Madame Q's girls?" Minerva asked. I didn't know who Madame Q was, but I could guess.

"No. I'm self made."

Lily took a few sips of weak tea. Not much, but she'd take no more.

"Lily," I pleaded. "Your body needs sustenance."

"You should have let me die." She closed her eyes, feigning sleep.

Min would let no one feel sorry for themself. Not even the half dead waif I rescued from the street. "Poppycock. If you wanted to die, she'd have found your corpse. I'm not sure what it is that has you all fired up to live, but you damn well did."

With effort, Lily swallowed. "I escaped him."

Minerva and I matched gazes across Lily's bed.

"Lily," I began. "Do you know who did this to you?"

She shook her head. "He put a cloth over my head and tied me up. Threw me into a cart, he did. Took me someplace and...did what he did. He said he had big plans for me. Experiment he said. Said something about how my life wasn't worth much, but my death would benefit mankind. Like the other girls. He wore a mask."

I shivered. Was he the same animal that had taken Shelby? "Your life is worth much more than he said." She didn't believe me. "When you're feeling better, Lily, maybe we can figure out who he is. Make him pay.

She snorted. "I didn't see him, but he was quality I tell you. Nobody is going to make him pay for taking a whore. He took me to a cabin in the woods. I got that bag off my head. God, why didn't I just leave it on? There was blood, so much blood. And this monster...it was some kind of zombie, I swear to God. It was the last thing I saw." She closed her eyes. "I'm tired. So tired."

We excused ourselves and let her rest.

"A zombie?" I repeated once we were back downstairs. "Do you think he drugged her?"

"I certainly hope so."

The drinks I'd down churned in my stomach like a wheel of knives. "Do you think it's the same that killed Shelby? That maybe he's got bodies...Oh God."

I collapsed into a chair and tried to keep the contents of my stomach in place.

Min put a cool rag on my forehead. "I'll make an anonymous tip to a constable I'm friendly with. Maybe it's the clue they've been waiting for."

Except both of us knew they weren't really waiting on any clues. Solving the murders wasn't high on anyone's list of priorities. Except maybe ours.

When my stomach settled, Min told me I'd best get home before I got into any more trouble.

The problem was that trouble seemed to be everywhere I looked.

Chapter Eleven

IT WAS ONLY a night later that brought yet another ghost to Thornfield.

"Where is she?" Gideon's voice boomed from the entryway. "Violet! Violet where are you?"

I stood warily from my perch at the kitchen table where I'd been keeping vigil with Claire and Jeannette, his shouts thundering through the house as he closed in on my whereabouts. He slid into the room, spinning in a typhoon of dark emotion, his hair in disarray, his unbuttoned coat flying behind him like a sail.

He stopped dead in his tracks, panting and red-eyed. "Violet," he said simply, my name a prayer on his lips as if he hadn't just roiled through the night to find me.

"Yes, Mr. Winston?" I glanced at the two maids I'd been sharing tea with, hoping they didn't deduce too much familiarity from Gideon's manner. "What can I do for you?"

His jaw clenched and his throat worked mightily around words that would not form. "There is a problem. Come with me."

Not waiting for me to comply he steered me to the door by my elbow.

"Is it Phillip? Is Phillip all right?"

My feet barely touched the floor as he herded me into the first empty room he came across, closing and locking the door behind us.

"Gideon, is Phillip well? You're scaring me."

"I'm scaring you?" He shoved me against the door and took my lips in crazed ravishment, his arms like iron bands holding me still. The dark storm seized us both, throwing us overboard into a heady sea as he kissed and kissed me.

As if he were suddenly spent, he slumped against me, breathing into my neck, pulling the pins from my hair.

"Gideon?" He didn't answer but for the hoarse breaths he drew. "Gideon, did you know...had you heard? Marisol has gone missing."

"Marisol," he said into my skin. He shuddered, great racking quakes that shook us both. "They found a body, Violet. They said...they said they'd never seen anything like it. They found it in pieces."

Bile threatened, churning in my stomach, making me take deep breaths. "Marisol?" I whispered.

"I don't know." He raised his head and examined me as if committing my face to memory. "I was standing at a street vendor when I overheard two constables talking about their gruesome find. One said he thought she was a maid from Thornfield." He paused and began to shake anew. "I didn't know Marisol was missing, Violet. I went crazy thinking it might be you."

"Oh, Gideon." I pulled his head to my chest and stroked his hair, whispering into the downy softness of it. "I'm fine. I'm here."

He squeezed me as if to prove I was really there, in his arms. "I couldn't...God, Violet. I barely remember getting here. I couldn't take the time to even call. I was afraid....afraid that if I didn't see you for myself, that if I tempted fate with the question, then surely the answer would be you."

"Shh." I held him close and we slid down the door. He laid his head in my lap and I stroked his locks, whispering nonsense words to comfort us both from a truth that would not find relief.

The world had gone mad, but this time, this time I had someone I could hold on to.

When he was calmer, he checked the hall for witnesses and led me to my chambers, locking the door behind him. He undressed me so carefully, as if I were made of porcelain and my clothes fragile silk. He stepped back and explored me with his eyes, my skin heating everywhere his gaze touched me.

"Is it right to do this tonight?" I asked. It was never right, but felt disrespectful, somehow, to Marisol.

"We have to find grace where we can, sprite." He was more ruthless with his own attire, and by then I was grateful for him to speed up.

I needed to feel him naked against me, naked inside me. I needed it like I needed air.

Gideon didn't, however, speed things up. A calm had prevailed over him, the quiet eye of the tempest, and he kissed me sweetly, tempering my heat with his cool. I arched into him, willing him into my body, but he took his time, murmuring sweet words into my skin, imprinting what had been mine into his. When at last he entered me, he did so achingly slow. He held my hands pinioned to the pillow on either side of my head, and he looked into my eyes and he held us in that infinite moment without moving.

I'm afraid I gave him everything then. My eyes betrayed the things I'd left unsaid, and he took it all in, knowing me in a way I'd been trying to hold back.

"Jesus, Violet, you're the heart before the break."

I couldn't ask what he meant, for he began to move slowly, deliciously between my thighs, and I gave up the worries that tethered me to this world so I could fly with him on another. Time held us in a place apart from the rest. There was only the slide of skin, the heat of love, and the crash of souls.

I watched him as he let go, all the powerful man and beast roaring into the night. And when he returned to me, he laid battle weary on my chest. I couldn't imagine returning to what we once knew for I was changed...he was changed. We'd ripped down the seam of our world, tearing the stitches out, never once thinking what would become of us without the very fabric of our lives.

"There you are."

I found Gideon in the library pouring himself a drink. He turned, glass in hand. It was filled near to the top, not the two to three fingers most gentlemen used. I blinked my surprise, but made no comment.

I made sure the door was closed firmly behind me. It had been two days since Gideon had made love to me last. I tried to remember I had no claim to his time, but I missed him.

I crossed the room, conscious that my drab brown dress covered all the parts that might entice him. "I have a free day coming up. I thought I might visit the cemetery. Shelby's employer paid for a marker. I wondered if you'd like to go with me."

He said nothing for a long time and shook his head. "I don't think so."

"It wouldn't be prudent, I know," I answered, trying to swallow back against the rising of my heart in my chest. Something was wrong. "I didn't mean we should leave the house together. I thought perhaps you could meet me."

"I'm sure John will be happy to take you."

His words were a slap in the face. "Why would John go with me?"

Gideon downed half his drink in an angry swallow. "He's sweet on you, surely you can see that? He'd be a better companion for such a thing."

I tread carefully across the words he'd thrown out, searching for an accusation or an explanation of what had troubled him so. "John is my friend, but it's your company I was seeking."

"Did you know that my father hates women?" It seemed a rhetorical question, so I waited for more. "He hated my mother most of all. She died giving birth to Phillip, but what nobody ever says is that she gave birth at the bottom of the stairs." He stared into the fire grate, though no fire was set. "He thinks all women are whores. I remember him saying that to her more than once."

"Gideon—"

"I don't think that's true, but I do believe that all men are bastards. Especially me. I'm the worst kind. I pretend I'm different when I'm not. I'm a right bloody bastard, just like him."

He was scaring me. "Perhaps I'll leave you to your brandy and we can speak later."

My hand was on the door. "It's over, Violet."

I didn't move, didn't turn, didn't breathe. "I see."

"Do you? Do you understand what I'm saying?"

I pivoted with the handle of my escape firm in my grip. The color rose and fell in my face as the heat prickled into ice that first covered my skin, then journeyed inward. "I take your meaning, sir."

I thought I felt cold, but it was nothing compared to the expression on Gideon's face. "Well, you always were a smart girl."

Nay, not a smart girl. A very foolish one. I'd risked my career for a chance to touch the stars, but forgot that they were light already dead. I let my chin have its due, thrusting proudly as if the world weren't caving in around us. "Were you expecting histrionics then?"

He laughed that sharp, mirthless noise he makes in the company of those he holds no respect for. "I should have known better. No smelling salts for our Miss Merriweather." He downed the rest of his chosen poison. "Though my pride may require a tear, I'm glad of your pragmatism."

His pride. His pride? And what of mine? Was I to have none? Of course not. This was what I earned by allowing my pride and heart to reign my sense. I was a servant. A woman. An orphan. I'd had the good fortune of a station in a good home, and I threw it away to dally with my employer. "Perhaps the next governess can hold your attention longer."

Gideon shook his head. "There will be no new governess. Your position here is safe. Nobody need know."

Every word from his mouth transferred more frost to my heart, so I decided to keep him talking. The more encased in ice it was, the less likely it would ever thaw again, and that was my new goal. "The way you bellowed my name through the manor the other night made sure that the household does indeed know something. It won't be long before I'm gone, Gideon. At least you won't have to be reminded of your mistake at every meal, though, right?"

"I am your mistake, not the other way around, Violet."

None of it made sense. The last time we'd been together, he'd been unraveled with need. How could he change his feelings like a new shirt? I wanted to ask, wanted to beg for explanation, really, but would not. I would learn my lesson from this and learn it well. I'd promised myself after Shelby's death never to allow another into my heart and look what I'd almost done. Had any more time passed on our love affair, surely I would have fallen in love with him, and then where would I be?

"If that is all then, Mr. Winston?"

He narrowed his eyes at me in a thinly veiled glare as if I were the one causing this scene. He shook his head berating himself in an argument taking place where only he could hear. He turned back to his precious decanter to refill the ache that no human alive could do for him. "Marry John, Violet. It won't take much. A few smiles, a fleeting glance or two. He'll fall over himself to secure your future."

"John deserves a woman who loves him. As it happens, I am barren in more ways than one."

I didn't cry as I quietly left the room. Not one tear. Not that night or any night after. Gideon would simply have to find another way to heal his wounded pride.

If Minerva was surprised to see me on my next free day, she didn't show it.

I handed her a parcel.

"What's this," she asked.

"Lily's belongings."

She cocked her head for a better explanation.

"A dress, some coin, a very old, yet still working PEAD, and a letter of recommendation from her last employer. Everything she'll need to get a fresh start once she's regained some of her health."

Min's eyebrows made extravagant arches over her eyes. "You forged a letter of recommendation?"

I didn't answer. I didn't have to. If my treachery were discovered, losing my job would be the least of my problems.

I ran my finger over the shiny wood of the bar. "I can't come back here. After today. I trust you'll do the best you can for Lily." It was Gideon's world. I had been an interloper. It was time to return to the life I was meant to live.

Minerva pushed a cup of tea towards me. "So you finally threw him over then."

"Not exactly." I looked up into her disbelieving eyes. "Don't look so surprised. Surely I'm not the first, nor the last, in line for his affections."

"He never brought anyone here before."

I shrugged. "He shouldn't have brought me. I'm not suited to the environment. I'm too staid."

"You're an idiot, anyway."

"Min!"

She lifted one shoulder casually, as if she couldn't be bothered to shrug both. "Well, you both are. You never should have risked it, either of you. But I'll tell you one thing, Miss Prim, no woman ever shared his bed more than once. Not before you, and if his moping the last few nights is any indication, it won't happen after you either."

Of course she knew all along we were lovers, but it didn't stop the blush from blooming on my cheeks to be reminded of sharing his bed. "It's none of my business how he spends his time."

"Do you love him?"

"No," I answered quickly. If she were picking me apart, which I'm sure she was, she would probably say too quickly. But she let it go.

"You're still welcome here. It's my ribaldery, not Gideon's."

I put my hand over hers for the briefest of moments. I hoped it was enough to convey how much her words meant to me. "It's too dangerous for me. I need to blend back into the walls of Thornfield and hope I didn't draw too much attention to myself. To you."

She nodded. "I'll take care of Lily. Don't worry about her."

That was as emotional as our goodbye would get, for neither Minerva nor the governess could risk feeling any more than that.

Chapter Twelve

A LOUD THUMP jolted me awake. I blinked at the darkness while my heart punched a crazy, irregular beat against my ribcage that couldn't be good for me. I listened intently and the noise repeated. It was above my head, in the attic. It had to be. Had an animal somehow found its way in to avoid the harsh winter?

Even as I pretended not to know better, my ears stayed on alert. And then I heard the scream. It was muffled quickly. Cut short. I choked on my breath as ice replaced the blood in my veins. There was no denying or explaining it away any longer. Something nefarious was happening, and I could no longer ignore that it was happening right above my head.

Not bothering to turn the dial on my bedside lamp, I swung my legs over the bed and grabbed my wrap from the foot of the bed. I wanted to light every lamp in the room but knew that it wouldn't change what was happening in the dark of night. Something foul lived in the walls of Thornfield Abbey. It had mocked me with its secrets long enough.

My slippers were warm, but provided no comfort. I tightened the sash of my robe and inhaled as deep a breath as my lungs would allow as I opened the secret panel. I wished that Gideon were home, before I remembered he'd not aid me in any case. Instead of going left, I took the unfamiliar right. The wall torches became scarcer the further I traveled, but I remembered that they came off the wall and removed one to be my guide.

The dark, narrow corridor curved and curled into a confused path as I went up and up. The sensation of fear was powerful, but my will was stronger. For better or worse, I was committed to ending the mystery that held the Winstons in its clutches with talons like a hawk holding a mouse.

The hall was damp and fusty, spreading a vague sense of ill into my very bones. I don't think a cloak of fur could have warmed me by that point. Reaching the dead end, my facade of bravery cracked. What was wrong with me? Why in world had I gone on this errand alone? I could have trapped myself in the walls never to be seen again. Maybe some other hapless person had done the same and it was their ghost I kept hearing in my slumber. It occurred to me I deserved whatever would befall me for putting myself in danger.

I didn't see any mechanisms in the wall like the one that opened the secret door of my room. Finally I noticed an empty torch holder and placed my light in the holster so I could better investigate. As soon as it clicked into place, the wall opened revealing a laboratory similar to John's on the lower level.

I stepped in and the wall closed behind me. The sound of it reminded me of the noise that had awoken me. As I moved further into the lab, the comparisons to John's workplace stopped. Tables glowed with tubes and beakers of glowing viscous liquids of differing colors. The bubbling sounds gurgled ominously, though I couldn't say why the sound bothered me. A jar of congealed...something...made me queasy and my dinner threatened to make a reappearance.

I explored the lab some more and found each jar held something more disgusting than the last. An entire shelf was full of glass containers of what looked like organs, and the shelf below it contained the same lumps of flesh, only they were mutated into shapes unnatural and gruesome. My skin pulled tightly into gooseflesh. What kind of experiments were these and who was performing them?

There was still no sign of whoever had made the screaming noise or the one who had muffled it. I knew better than to let that appease my fear. Just because they hadn't shown themselves did not remove the danger. There was an actual door at the far end of the laboratory and every instinct told me not to approach it.

The hair on the back of my neck quilled in warning. It was on the other side of the door I would find my answers. I swallowed. But how badly did I want them?

I thought of Shelby. Had she met her end in this very room? Or maybe the cabin in the woods? Trepidation would not save the next poor woman from a violent death, and so I imagined an iron stake as my spine and pushed the door open slowly. My heart seized and pushed my blood through my veins incorrectly at the sight of a woman strapped to a vertical table. She didn't look well. In fact, it appeared she may have met her end some time ago. Part of her exposed skin was the color of mold but it also looked like parts of her were made of copper plates and wires.

There was nothing to fear from the dead, I reminded myself. There was nobody else in the room. I approached the table, sickened and heartbroken at the departed soul. How long had she been in this room? Why had her body not been put to rest? What nefarious purpose could she be serving?

Here was Lily's zombie.

I swallowed the bile inching up my throat and stepped closer. She was attached to a hulking machine with tubes and wires. In the center of it, an overlarge bellow expanded and contracted with hisses and puffs. I looked at her face, trying to discern...I don't know what I hoped for...an approximate age or something.

Evidence of an easy life or death would not be found in her appearance as she was something in between the two. Half of her face was mottled skin of purple, green, and blue. The other half was a polished copper skull. She looked familiar, though, despite her fiendish manifestation.

Oh, dear God.

I took a step back.

No. No. No.

The woman on the table was Elizabeth Winston. Gideon, John, and Phillip's mother. Their very dead mother.

As soon as I made the connection, Mrs. Winston opened her eyes.

I screamed. It was like looking into the eyes of hell. Those eyes—I would never sleep again without seeing those deranged, tortured eyes.

Mrs. Winston moaned, and I screamed again.

Dear Lord, how had this happened?

"Violet, are you in here?" John's voice called from the other chamber.

Oh, poor John. I couldn't let him see his mother. Not like this. He called again and it spurred me to run out of the room. I didn't stop until I reached him, and then I propelled myself into his arms. "Oh, John"

"Violet, are you all right?" He held me close, probably trying to discern how to help me. John was always so caring. He didn't deserve this.

The Colonel was a monster. And he'd turned his wife into one as well. I was enraged and frightened at the same time. How could a person so sick manage to keep his true nature hidden for so long?

"Darling, you're shaking," John said into my hair. "What is it that has you so agitated?"

I pulled back to look into his face. The calm I found in his eyes made me feel even worse. That he should have to deal with yet another family tragedy was so unfair. "We must leave this room immediately, John."

"What is wrong?"

I shook my head. "We have to call the authorities." I pulled him toward the entrance, but he refused to budge.

"What did you see, Violet? Is there something on the other side of that door?" He started that direction.

"No," I cried. "You must not enter that vile room. Please, John. You must trust me. There is nothing on the other side of that door but heartbreak." I pulled harder, but he was stalwart in his direction. "It's awful. Your father...he has done something atrocious but I cannot allow you to see it. Please, I beg you. Please just come out of here with me. We'll let the authorities deal with this."

"It must be bad, Vi. You're in your nightclothes. What propelled you out of your bed at this hour?"

He wasn't taking me seriously. Of course, I must have appeared a hysterical wreck. There was no help for that as it was an understatement of my condition. "John, we must go. Please."

"How did you even find this place?"

I began to cry then. Fat tears that served no purpose and would not get us out of there. "I heard noises. I'm afraid he will come back. Please, we have to leave now."

"Who will come back, Violet?"

"The Colonel!" I turned towards the exit, but John pulled me back into his chest.

"I daresay the Colonel will not find you here," he said. One of his arms banded around me tightly.

I was trapped with my back against him. If he thought to calm me down, caging me was doing the opposite. "Please loosen your grip, John. I can hardly breathe."

He kissed my cheek. "That could pose a problem, my love." He held a handkerchief to my nose. "For I need you to take several very deep breaths right now."

I couldn't move away from the sweet smelling kerchief for I was pinned in place. I didn't understand what was happening as I began to get woozy. I was so very tired, and suddenly, falling asleep in John's arms was very appealing indeed. I felt myself let go, then, even as part of me raged to stay awake. I drifted into beautiful oblivion.

I danced in the clouds. A nagging voice told me to stop, to return to Thornfield. I had work to do—Phillip had a lesson I was to attend to. And yet, I danced. Gideon was there, dashing as ever, and he took me into his arms and we flew as if the world had no cares.

"You should wake up, sprite," he said to me.

"I like you better when you don't speak, Gideon," I retorted, and he laughed.

We dipped and twirled until my stomach was unsettled and my head ached. I began coughing and my dreamscape changed. Gideon was gone and I was left with the sour tummy and blistering head. I couldn't move, my frozen limbs covered in snow.

I blinked. No. Not frozen. Tied down. I was tethered to a table in the lab. I blinked some more. Oh dear God, John. John had done this.

As if I summoned him, his face came into view. "Ho, there she is," he said jovially. "I was beginning to wonder if I'd misjudged my tincture. You must be in an awful way right now, and for that I'm sorry. Usually, I don't wake my subjects up at this point, but you...you are special."

"John, what is going on? Why are you doing this?"

He had a syringe in his hands that he tapped several times. I squeezed my eyes closed, but he injected the contents into his own arm. He looked euphoric for a moment, and then his normal countenance returned. "I'm sorry. Did you ask me something?"

He was mad. There was no other explanation. "I asked you why you are doing this."

"Typical Violet. Most people would ask to be released, beg for forgiveness. Not our governess, of course. She wants to know why...why? Why? Why? Haven't you learned by now that ours is not to question why?" His smile was affable, but his eyes were tinged with manic zeal. "I wouldn't have you any other way, my dear." He paused. "Wait! Yes, I would." He closed the distance between us, bringing his face inches before mine. "I would have rather had you not be a whore."

I gasped.

"Oh, don't pretend to be puritanical with me. I know all about you and Gideon. In fact, I've watched you." He whispered into my ear, "The walls have eyes, Miss Merriweather."

"You watched me?"

He barked a harsh laugh. "I bet you wish you could have kept your legs closed now, don't you?"

I winced. It was like a stranger had taken over the body of my friend. Each of his words was laced with unstable anger. The thought of him watching me with Gideon made me want to wretch.

"My mother was a whore, too, Violet. But I think I can fix her. Really. I'm getting closer all the time." He retreated a few feet away from me, but I didn't know what he was about.

I tried to reason with him. "Your mother died."

"More or less," he agreed.

Was there a way out of this situation? Once again, I cursed my impetuous nature. I thought that keeping him talking would either give me more time to find an escape or would give him more time to unhinge completely.

"You see, she died in a sense...but science, science is a wonderful thing. I've kept her less than alive but more than dead for many years."

Less than alive but more than dead? "What does that mean?"

"It means I'm going to fix her. She will not die a whore—she'll be reborn and live the life she was meant to live. Be who she was meant to be. And you are going to help her, you selfless, wonderful girl."

Chapter Thirteen

I DID NOT like the sound of that at all, and I struggled against the binds. "Please, John. Undo these straps. Let's go downstairs and have a cup of tea and find a solution. I want to help you. Really, I do. But not like this."

"A cup of tea?" John scoffed. "Oh my goodness, you really are delusional, aren't you?"

I wasn't the only delusional person in the room, but I didn't dare voice that. "What are you going to do to me?"

"Mommy needs flesh. Flesh and blood to survive. You won't be needing yours much longer, so you'll donate to Mommy."

I sobbed.

He kissed me hard on the mouth and then went back to his machines. It was then I thought of Gideon and his kisses, how it was likely I would never have another. I'd never see his face again, never tease him, never argue. Though we'd been at odds lately, a part of me thought we had all the time in the world to make it up. How foolish. I would die here and they'd never find my body. I'd just be one more ghost to haunt Thornfield. One more lost chance to Gideon.

I believed he would mourn me. I hoped he'd be there for Phillip, who would not understand my disappearance. Poor Phillip. What would become of him now? He would be another victim of Thornfield, where hate lived in the pockets of shadow and overtook the light at every opportunity. I ached to be able to ruffle his hair one more time. To leave him with at least the knowledge that he was loved like a son.

I squeezed my eyes. A son. I'd never thought I'd have children of my own. I had resolved to a lifetime of caring for other people's children. I didn't expect that I would be so moved by a tiny hand clutching my skirt. I didn't know I had the capacity for a mother's love.

For Phillip, I would beg. "Please, John. I don't want to die. Phillip needs me."

"You've done enough damage to my family already. Phillip doesn't need a jezebel like you confusing him. Besides, before too long, he'll have our mother back and you'll be nothing but a memory. For all of us."

He couldn't have cleaved my heart in two as efficiently with a knife than he just did with his words.

"Because I'm just a nameless governess, right? I mean nothing to anyone. Like the other women you've killed?"

John rolled my bed to the machine attached to his mother. "Is this the part where I confess to all my nefarious deeds? Will it balm your departing soul to hear them? Maybe make your journey into the afterlife a little easier? Fine, Violet. I abducted the servants and used them to keep my mother alive."

"Used them? You mean killed them?"

"It was their life or my mother's. Frankly, I don't think the courts would convict me. Not that they'll ever know. You certainly won't be able to tell them anything."

I could see her from my new vantage point. She was watching me. Those frenzied, demonical eyes. "Why does she need flesh and blood?"

"I've been able to keep her mostly alive, yet she is still technically a decomposing corpse. As parts of her body die, I must graft new flesh—flesh of a living person—to her. I tried to use the skin of the recently departed when I first started—but it doesn't last nearly as long. Hardly worth the hassle of robbing graves."

I shuddered. Did she know what was happening to her? Was she aware of the heinous monster she had become? "And the...donor...must die?"

"Well, you see, I've perfected the process. Mother also needs blood transfusions periodically. Large amounts of blood, mind you. I've been able to acquire the flesh while I drain the blood and then, well, there isn't much left of the donor."

He was odious. All this time, I'd been living with a devil, and I was going to die at his hands. A horrible death. The kind of death most people couldn't dream up in their worst nightmares. And Gideon had thought John to be the better brother. The trustworthy, stalwart one. It hurt to know that everyone else agreed with him most of the time, and would continue to do so while John carried on with his lunatic experiments and his mad killing sprees.

"You have a special distinction, though, my dear Violet. You are going to also help me test my inVirtuator chip." He held up a brass square. "If I insert this into your brain...you will no longer feel any sexual longing at all. In fact, even thinking about the act will send neuron impulses through your brain that register pain and loathing."

"Why are you going to test it on me if you are going to kill me?"

"To see if it works. I can't very well test it on my mother." He clucked as if I were the one talking crazy. "You see, I'll put this into your brain, and then we'll have sexual congress, in the name of science of course. If all goes according to my hypothesis, you will beg me to kill you while we're joined. You will hate every second of it, of course, and it will be extremely painful."

He was going to defile me—first with an aberrant mechanism in my brain, and then he meant to rape me. He may have deluded himself that this was for science, but it was really because he hated women. His mother most especially.

"If it works, I'm going to put it in Mother so she'll be good. And then, why I may sell the inVirtuator to men saddled with their own whores. Think of it, Violet, your gift to science will improve the lives of so many."

"You're insane!" I cried.

"No, not really. My reasoning is quite sound. Women who are whores abandon their children. They ruin everyone's lives—especially their own. This inVirtuator will save New Geneva."

"I am not a whore. A woman who enjoys sex is not a whore. She is a woman—the way God made her." My rage was as hot as my fear was cold. "Women have as much right to enjoy the pleasure of life as men have. All of the pleasures since we share all of the pain and burden, do we not?"

"A man doesn't leave his children to satisfy his baser cravings. That's what she was doing, my mother. The day she died, she was saying goodbye to her children. She was going to leave us all to take up with her paramour. Her love life couldn't be intruded upon by children. It was the second time she was leaving me for a man who was not my father—do you think that is how God made her?" John's face was bright red, and the veins in his forehead protruded violently.

"I'm not saying your mother was right to abandon you, but all women can't be painted with the same brushstroke."

"You cannot mean to say that being my brother's lover and risking everything you hold dear was not a mistake. You let your sexual notions dictate your choices. Was it worth it? The fleeting romance? He left you, didn't he? You risked everything and he left you anyway."

"It wasn't just sexual notions," I protested.

"What was it, then? Love?" He scoffed.

"Yes!" I shouted, surprising myself. "I loved him. I still love him." And it was true. "I would do it again. What we had was beautiful. It wasn't sordid or ugly, and we hurt no one else by finding solace in each other's arms." How I wished I'd said the same to Gideon when I had the chance.

"If you could have controlled your libido, you wouldn't be here right now. Still think your pleasure trumps all?" He tied a tourniquet around my arm. "I fancied myself in love with you for a time. We could have been married by now. Perhaps starting a family of our own. Gideon would never have offered for you."

The thought of willingly marrying John made me as sick as his promises of violence. Still, agitating him further wasn't in my best interests. "Is your mother aware of what is happening to her?" I risked a glance at the battered body staring at me with an unholy glee.

"She's in there somewhere. Once I get the inVirtuator in place, I'll work out the rest of her mind. It will be hard for her to get used to being part robotic and part human, but I'll be there for her." He tapped on my arm, bidding my veins to come to him. "I'm going to give you a mild tranquilizer. I'll need you to be somewhat coherent during the surgery."

He was going to crack my head open and poke my brains while I was awake? I began keening and begging him for mercy. I didn't even know what I was saying.

"Stop this!" a voice thundered. The unlikeliest of voices, for I recognized it to be the Colonel.

I couldn't see him, but I could gauge by John's paler face that he wasn't expecting him to find this room.

"What in God's name is going on here?" the older man blustered. "My God, John, what have you done?"

"Father I can explain—"

The Colonel shook his cane at the abomination. "What is that?"

"Father—"

"Miss Merriweather, what are you doing in here?" Recrimination laced his concern. As if I had done this to myself somehow.

"Please, Colonel, untie me."

"What have you done, John?"

"Not another step, Father, or I inject this poison into Violet's heart."

My eyes flew to the syringe in his hand.

John pat my arm as if consoling a small child. "The tincture will not kill you if I put it into your veins slowly, however, this dose straight into your heart would be fatal."

"Why would you want to kill the governess? I thought you were trying to win her favor. What the devil is going on?"

It was awful being so helpless. I trusted that neither man really cared about my fate one way or the other. I'd tried appealing to John's basic human empathy to no avail. The Colonel's might not run any deeper, knowing how he felt about women and servants in general. That my fate lie solely in their hands—had always, in fact, been in the hands of men who cared not for me as a person, enraged me. I had been powerless since I was born—my small rebellions had not changed anything for anyone, much less myself.

There was a brass button on the apparatus that billowed air into Mrs. Winston's machine. I didn't know what it did, but it seemed like a fairly good distraction, so while John tried to placate the Colonel, I stretched, ignoring the searing pain of muscle, until my finger hit the button. A screeching siren sounded.

"You bitch!" John yelled, dropping the syringe and scurrying around my table to set to rights whatever I'd accomplished. The Colonel picked up the syringe and pocketed it while he began unstrapping me.

"Father, no. If you'll only let me explain."

"Explain? Explain to me that my son has abducted the governess and is doing fiendish experiments in league with the devil?"

I sat up in time for the Colonel to get his first good look at his wife.

"My God." He paled considerably. "Is that...what have you done, John?"

The Colonel clutched his chest. John looked at me in blame, taking strides toward the table. I hopped off it and pushed it so that it rolled into him. I tried to run around it, but he grabbed me by my middle as I passed. The Colonel, still in the throes of heart pain, had stumbled up to the living corpse.

"Elizabeth...oh my Elizabeth. What has he done to you?"

She began an awful keening sound. It wasn't human, the noise that emanated from her throat. The despair and horror should not have been born.

The Colonel, shaking, began to unbind her.

"Father, no!" John let go of me in the rush to stop his father. I searched for a weapon, lest I not make it to the door again. A bloody butcher knife dripping in an unknown source of gore sat on a block and I took it, pushing down the rising bile in my throat. I couldn't afford to be sickened or frightened. My life was in my hands. The lives of countless other future victims also depended on stopping John and his sordid experiments.

John pushed his father away from Elizabeth Winston and they both went down to the floor. The monster that used to be a wife and mother saw me and howled, shambling towards me with a super human speed. I screamed as she grabbed my shoulder and howled in my face.

Her grasp crushed against my bone, causing me to slump. She shook me like a rag doll and stared into my eyes as her lips slipped off her face and on onto the floor. She kept saying the same syllables over and over until I recognized that she was trying to form words.

Words. Words from a corpse. Dear Lord, she was sentient.

"What? What do you want?" I cried. When would this nightmare end?

"Kay may! Kay may!" And she looked at my knife with what I can only describe as longing.

Kill me. Kill me.

She wanted me to put her out of her misery.

"You want me to kill you?" I asked.

"Kay may!" she affirmed.

I raised my knife but hesitated.

"Kay may!"

"Violet, no. Please." John had left his father on a pile of the floor. "Please, don't."

John seemed suddenly like himself, like the friend I'd counted on. I knew it wasn't real, but if there was any part of him left in what he'd become...could I help him?

"I need to get her back on the machine. If I don't, she'll decompose quickly. Please, it will be agonizing for her."

Her mottled skin was sliding around and her stench was becoming unbearable. I lowered the knife. He would likely bring her to life again anyway. What used to be Mrs. Winston cried out and grabbed my wrist tightly, impaling herself on the knife.

Over and over she used my hand to stab her own heart...well, maybe it wasn't her heart. Maybe it was Shelby's heart, or Marisol's, or any of the nameless women he'd stolen. Her grip became looser and she fell to the floor in a heap. I dropped the knife in time to see John fly at me with eyes red with rage.

He dove into me and a shot rang out. He shook my shoulders, as his mother had, and then he crumpled to the floor on top of her, a round bullet hole in his back.

The Colonel held the smoking gun pointed at me.

Chapter Fourteen

THE COLONEL'S HAND shook, but he did not lower the gun.

I stepped back without taking my eyes from him.

From the doorway, Gideon called my name. "Violet?"

I wished I could keep him out. I didn't want him to see all the blood and carnage of his family.

"Father?"

The Colonel snapped out of his trance and lowered the gun. I turned slowly. I saw the play of so many emotions cross Gideon's face as he looked at me. "I heard a gunshot." He was oddly transfixed to his spot in the door. "Sprite," his voice broke on my name. "Please tell me you're all right."

I looked down at the blood coating my robe. I took a step towards him, but my legs shook badly, and the world began to tilt. Gideon ran to me, clutching me tightly and holding me from a fall. I could scarcely draw breath, he held me so hard.

I clung to him, twisting his shirt in my hands in an effort to make myself inextricable. "Don't let me go."

"I'm never letting you out of my sight again."

I pulled back enough to see his face. My dark rogue. The safest place I'd ever been. "I love you. I should have told you before. I know you don't want my love, but you have it anyway. I'm not asking for you to change, I swear. You only need know that you have my heart."

I kissed him. I kissed him with all the love I'd thought I could never feel, with all the hope I thought I didn't have.

"Marry me," he said against my lips.

I pulled back. "Marry?"

"I can't think of anything I want more than to be shackled to you for the rest of my life. At least then maybe I'll have a chance of keeping you out of trouble."

"Don't wager on it," I whispered and kissed him again.

Hours later, in my room, Gideon was quietly concentrating while he stripped the bloody gown from me and helped me into the tub.

"You shouldn't be in here. Half the house is awake."

"My brother is a homicidal psychopath who's been shot by my father. I don't think anyone in this house gives two figs if I attend to my fiancé's bath. Are you sure you're all right?"

I sank deeper into the bubbles. "If I don't think about anything I saw, I'm fine." Fiancé. "I won't hold you to it, you know. If you change your mind after the crisis has passed. You needn't marry me."

"Violet—"

"I didn't tell you I loved you to force your hand. I told you because I realized that if my life were to be cut short, I wanted you to know."

He winced. "I don't want to think about a life without you in it." He held my hand and kissed my scraped knuckles. "I know you say you're a governess, but I'm sure you've put some kind of hex on me. You're all the things I never wanted tied up in a sturdy, serviceable, gray bow and I'm prostrate at your feet with longing for them."

I didn't want to interrupt, which was rare when it came to Gideon, but I was enjoying listening to him fillet his heart open to me.

"When I saw you tonight, covered in all that blood, I went mad for a moment. I never want to come that close to losing you again, Vi. But, I should warn you, it's you who'll get the poor end of this bargain. I haven't a clue how to be a husband. I'll muck it up, that much I'm sure of. I don't deserve you."

I reached a sudsy hand to his face. "Everyone deserves love. You're actually the one who taught me that."

"Me?"

"When I came to this house, I believed that I had a station in life that was below other people…people like your family. You showed me a life where people accepted each other. Women are equal to men, rich are equal to poor. You taught me to value myself."

"You're better than anyone I know, Violet."

"Not better. More stubborn, perhaps."

He kissed the top of my head. "I know I hurt you when I pushed you away. I'm sorry. I realized I was getting in over my head with you. I thought it would be easier on my heart to break things off before I ruined us both."

"I had told you I needed no promises."

"When I went crazy thinking you might have disappeared I knew I loved you. When I made love to you that night, I knew it and I wanted so badly to tell you. But the light of day reminded me that you deserved so much more than I was capable of giving." He huffed. "I thought you'd be better off with John. I'm so sorry that I pushed you away."

He rested his forehead on mine, and I closed my eyes, letting go of the pain best I could. There was light rapping at my bedroom door.

Gideon stood. "I'll see to it."

I blushed in the hot water, wondering what they would think of Master Gideon answering my door. And then I decided not to care. I was starting a new life now. There were no actual laws forbidding me a man in my chambers. I was tired of living by everyone's moral code but my own.

Gideon came back, holding a clean wrap. "I'm afraid we need to cut your bath short. We've been summoned by the Colonel."

The bath water felt suddenly cold. So much for my bravado.

Though it was not yet dawn, I dressed in my serviceable brown dress to meet the Colonel in his chambers. The frock felt a little more like armor than my nightclothes, and I doubted I would be returning to sleep any time soon.

On the way to the Colonel's wing, I made Gideon stop at the nursery to check on Phillip.

He'd slept through the entire debacle, even as the Constable and his men were still carrying on in the laboratory above us. I tucked the blanket around him snuggly, pleased that he could remain innocent a bit longer, but dreading the conversation we'd have to have tomorrow.

If I were still allowed to be his governess tomorrow.

Gideon held my hand through the halls, daring anyone who came upon us to say a word. As a champion, I couldn't have asked for a more stalwart one. It would be harder to face the rest of the world's censure than it would be the staff that relied on his family for their livelihood, however. A man of his station simply did not marry the governess, regardless of how many men may have tarried with one.

And then there was the Colonel.

We took a deep breath and entered his dark room.

The massive furniture was as imposing as the Colonel himself. It positively screamed that it was as immovable and resolute as its owner. The high ceilings and gargantuan pieces made a person feel small, insignificant. My breath hiccupped in my throat, and Gideon caught my hand and led me to his father.

The physician was still attending him, but the Colonel waved him out. "I'm fine."

"You had a heart attack, sir. You're not fine. You must rest, and I'd like to make an appointment to replace one of your artificial valves." The doctor looked to us. "I don't know why I bother, but if you can keep him calm, please do. Excitement isn't good for him."

"How is John?" Gideon asked, and I shuddered.

"The sanitarium is in charge of his care now," the doctor answered. "If they are able to remove the bullet, he'll likely make a full recovery. Unless of course the tincture he's been self-dosing has lasting side effects."

"Surely they won't release him," I cried, forgetting that his family may very well want him back.

Gideon's strong arm pulled me close. "He'll never get near you again, Violet."

The doctor shook his head. "I was referring to his physical rehabilitation, Miss Merriweather. It's doubtful that his mind is repairable."

The doctor made his farewells, and the Colonel waved us closer to his bedside. Though imposing, he wasn't nearly so bad when he was lying down and I was standing upright. Still he glowered at us and my heart picked up a swift chase in my ribcage.

"Father, you should be resting. We can talk tomorrow," Gideon said in his best imitation of respect.

"It's already tomorrow," the Colonel answered gruffly. "After they replace the faulty Atrioventiculator in my heart, I'm leaving Thornfield." He took on a faraway look that I was unaccustomed to seeing on the man. "There is a scouting mission for other suitable planets, and I've been asked to join. I'd thought to turn down the offer, but New Geneva cannot continue to grow without a plan for a sustainable future. We can't have another Earth, but more than that, I can't stay in this house another day. I'm leaving Thornfield to you, Gideon."

"Me?" Gideon asked incredulously. "What am I to do with an estate?"

"Learn to run it, I imagine," the Colonel replied. "You'll either run it to the ground or you'll learn some responsibility."

"And either way, you don't care, isn't that right?" Gideon remarked wryly.

"Gideon," I admonished.

"Pshaw, Miss Merriweather, let him speak his mind. He's been dying to for some time."

"I want nothing to do with this house."

"Then it can rot."

The men glowered at each other, no closer to repairing their relationship in the aftermath of the tragedy upstairs. Ever the pragmatic one, I thought of all the servants that would be displaced if the house was closed up. And though Gideon may not want it, there was Phillip to consider. It was his birthright also.

Phillip.

"What of Phillip, sir?" I asked.

"You'll have to ask the new master of the house. Phillip comes with Thornfield."

As if the boy were a vase or...or...a turnip. "And does the governess also come with Thornfield, sir? What of Oliver? And any other human beings on the premises?"

He narrowed his bushy brows. "Based on appearances, I assumed the governess would remain stodgily by the side of my second son. I'll leave it to you both to decide how to best deal with Phillip. Send him to a school, keep him here." He waved his hand to bat the pesky ideas away. "I haven't the gumption to bother caring any more. I did my best, these years, though I know you judge me harshly for it. She was never faithful, I'm not even sure John is truly mine, but I know for a fact Gideon and Phillip are not. I took responsibility for them, gave them my name and kept my wife untarnished. But I know I'm a cold man. Phillip will be better off without my influence. It seems I'm not the best father."

I wasn't expecting the admission. I suppose owning up to one's shortcomings was honorable, however, it seemed to me the better man would not just admit to them, but also try to change.

"I'm marrying Violet," Gideon said, the low, even challenge in his voice palpable.

"I can hardly stop you," the Colonel said.

"Would you want to?" I asked. "Is it such a blemish on your good name for Gideon to follow his heart?"

"Miss Merriweather, my good name is blemished beyond repair. I don't really care what you do. I have no use for any of you."

Though Gideon had long since realized that Colonel Winston had no love for him, hearing it aloud crushed him. I could see it in his eyes. A part of me wondered if he'd revert to his usual pattern of dealing with the disappointment. I hoped that earning my heart would be enough for him to realize his own worth. Gideon was a grown man, though, and it was Phillip I would concern myself with.

I started to say something to that effect when Gideon interrupted me. "We'll bid you good morning and see ourselves out."

He grasped my elbow, and if it hadn't been so important to show a united front, I would have balked. Instead I let him lead me out.

In the hall, servants passed us with trunks to pack up the Colonel. He certainly wasn't wasting any time. Gideon shushed me again as I started to speak.

"Stop doing that," I ground out. "I'll not be quieted. Not any longer. I'm quite tired of not being heard."

"Indulge me this once, sprite, and I'll endeavor to listen attentively from here on out for the rest of our days."

When he put it so nicely...

"We're keeping Thornfield."

"Well of course we're keeping Thornfield, Gideon. We can't very well let it rot."

"Let me finish, please."

I rolled my eyes. "Very well. But Phillip will be up soon, and we need to come up with a way to explain this night to the lad. We're keeping him as well." If I had to run away with the boy, he wouldn't be sent away to a cold, impersonal boarding school.

"I never entertained anything else."

"I'd like to move the academy here."

"Mrs. Witherspoon's Academy for Young Ladies of a Suitable Nature?"

The nonplussed expression on his face made me giggle, despite the horrid night's passing.

"That's the one, though perhaps we could shorten the name."

"I don't understand."

"Well, it's a bit cumbersome, don't you think?"

"Gideon!"

He smiled. "I want the world to be filled with women like you, Violet. I'd like you to lead an army of females into a brand new day."

"Gideon."

"I want to banish your ghosts," he added. "All the things that oppressed you, made you feel less than worthy, I want to blow them to smithereens."

"And what of your ghosts, Gideon?"

"You'll make short work of them, sprite. We'll fill this house full of children. Well fed, happy children. And you'll somehow make a family man of me. I won't have time to dwell on what lurks in the shadows when what's in the light is so much more appealing."

We stopped outside the nursery, knowing we'd have to go in shortly. "I hope you don't plan on being too good, Gideon. I rather fancy being married to a rogue."

"Violet, there's something else…"

My skin pricked at the foreboding in his words. "What is it Gideon?"

"It's the Juniper Society."

I felt my brows reach for the top of my head. "What about the Juniper Society?"

"It's quite humorous, actually…" The dubious expression on my face must have caused him to change his mind about that particular tactic. "Perhaps it's not quite as humorous as that."

"You're a member, aren't you?"

He gently rubbed the crease above my nose. "I'm one of the founding members, sprite. Though it was all Min's idea."

"I don't know why I hadn't guessed it. You're a perfect match for a band of gin-soaked marauders. I suppose you'll want to have your midnight meetings in the parlor now."

Once again, I found myself backed against a wall at Gideon's hand. "The only meetings I intend to hold at midnight will be in a four-post bed upstairs with my wife. However, gin-soaked afternoons once a week in the parlor might be nice."

"I doubt Minerva will attend anything during the light of day, but if what you're saying is that you want to legitimize the Junipers, I won't stand in your way."

"There's my girl," he said, right before his lips descended upon mine.

Newsletters are Sexy

Never miss a new release, special deal, sneak peak, or FREEBIES ever again. Don't worry, you can unsubscribe whenever you like and no spam is allowed. One <u>CLICK</u> and you're in. (And you get a free ebook!)

Ours is Just a Little Sorrow
Copyright © 2012 by Gwen Hayes
Don't Stop Believing
Copyright © 2015 by Gwen Hayes
All Rights Reserved

Don't miss out!

Click the button below and you can sign up to receive emails whenever Gwen Hayes publishes a new book. There's no charge and no obligation.

http://books2read.com/r/B-A-MTHB-XDTH

BOOKS 2 READ

Connecting independent readers to independent writers.

Also by Gwen Hayes

Silver Pines
Don't Stop Believing

Standalone
Second Son of a Duke
So Over You
Ours is Just a Little Sorrow
The Christmas Contradiction

Watch for more at www.gwenhayes.com.

About the Author

Gwen Hayes writes romance for adult and teen readers. You know...kissing books. She is represented by Jessica Sinsheimer at the Sarah Jane Freyman Literary Agency.

Gwen is also a romance editor at www.fresheyescritique.com because her dream job is to read books for a living.

Read more at www.gwenhayes.com.

Made in the USA
Charleston, SC
29 November 2015